REDBONE

ALSO BY RON BRIGGS

Yellow Hair Series

Erik Haraldsson

Tor's Saga

Cass

Westward

Journey to Iceland

Iceland

REDBONE

YELLOW HAIR
BOOK SEVEN

RON BRIGGS

WOLFPACK
PUBLISHING
— EST 2013 —

Redbone
Paperback Edition
Copyright © 2025 by Ron Briggs

Wolfpack Publishing
1707 E. Diana Street
Tampa, Florida 33609

www.wolfpackpublishing.com

This book is a work of fiction. References to historical events, real people, or real places are used fictitiously. Any similarity to real persons, living or dead, is purely coincidental and not intended by the author.

All brand names and product names used in this book are trademarks, registered trademarks, or trade names of their respective holders. Wolfpack Publishing is not associated with any product or vendor in this book.

Paperback ISBN 979-8-89567-143-6
Ebook ISBN 979-8-89567-142-9
LCCN 2025930886

FOREWORD

This is a work of fiction. The characters, events, and places are conceived of by the author. Any references to and actions by historical persons or places is fictionalized. An honest attempt has been made to describe real cultures and interactions as they may have taken place in the eleventh century CE.

With the story of Tor Eriksson and Heidi Torswife coming to a conclusion in the sixth segment of the series, we now focus on the characters left behind on Turtle Island. This segment will follow the son of Bright Star, Redbone. Readers will recall that Bright Star is the twin sister of Bright Moon. When Yellow Hair and Bright Moon left New Long Pine Village, Bright Star was pregnant with her first child by her husband, Red Hand.

During this time period, the metropolis known by the modern world as Cahokia blossomed into the largest prehistoric city north of Mexico, and its influence spread to encompass much of what is now eastern and southeastern North America. At the same time, the great cultural developments of the Ancestral Puebloans were in turmoil with shifting alliances, civil war, and political strife. In the northeast, Haudenosaunee groups were forming alliances, trying to establish nations, fighting among themselves, and with neighboring cultures.

REDBONE

CHAPTER 1
CHILDREN

"I still wish she had stayed here. There is still much to be done here to make New Long Pine Village a viable home for our three clans," Water Mint complained.

"Aunt, you know they had to get over the mountains to Sun Town before her baby comes," Bright Star defended her sister.

"He should have gone on without her if finding his people was so important. We need her strength and wisdom here as much as he needs a traveling companion to keep his blankets warm. He could come back after her in the summer when she would be ready for the dangerous and vigorous trail he was leading her on."

"Yes, we all miss her, but his timing in getting to that great Norse canoe is critical. There is no telling if the Norse will ever return to our shores. Bright Moon and Yellow Hair are being steered by forces that are out of our control. I just hope they are safe. She said Wolf told her it would be dangerous for her in Yellow Hair's world. I hope she finds peace and happiness. And I cannot wait for Red Oak to return with news of her little one."

When that statement left Bright Star's tongue, her own baby gave her a kick and started protracted movements within her womb. "This one is a restless one!" She pushed on the baby's foot that was pressed against her diaphragm, causing her shortness of breath.

"I think that one will be a warrior." Water Mint smiled at her niece.

It was the middle of the Cold Moon. Hunters were busy bringing meat to preserve for the long, winter moons to come. The days were short, and the women worked long hours preparing hides to make new, warm clothing, pounding corn into cornmeal for various dishes, boiling hominy for hungry mouths, cleaning roots, fruits, and nuts for making pemican and other foods, seeing after the needs of children, and trying to keep their husbands content. In addition, the clan matrons met frequently to assess needs and strategies for surviving the winter.

On top of all that was happening, Water Mint, Head Matron of the Water Plant Clan, and her niece, Bright Star, were feeling the effects of their advancing pregnancies. Water Mint's third child would arrive around the winter solstice, and Bright Star's first was due more than a moon later.

"Fingerling is of little help. All he wants to do is torment his sister and dominate my time. I think he is jealous of the new one. Tallow takes him when he can, but winter hunting is no place for a boy who has only seen six summers. Dewdrop is trying her best to be helpful, but her four summers limit her usefulness. Then she gets upset when her brother constantly teases her. And carrying this one is making for a challenging cold season," said Water Mint.

"I never realized how much trouble my sister and I were for our mother until I have watched you struggling with your children. It makes me wonder what I have to look forward to!" Bright Star quipped.

"Motherhood is a struggle, but we all seem to get through it. You will do just fine-you are stronger than me. In your head and your body. I should have trained with you and your sister when you were growing. I would be stronger today."

"You are joking. You were our rock and our comfort during all those seasons. We would have never gotten though it without you," Bright Star told her aunt.

"Hah, your sister was the rock. She did everything she said she would do, and you were right by her side!"

"And it was your hugs and steady support that we came back to at the end of the day. And, of course, the good meals and knowledge of plants were extremely helpful. Not to mention Tallow's hard but thorough training that got us through it all. It was a team effort, and we all played our part. Now, we have new roles to play. You are a great Head Matron, by the way. I do not know if you hear that enough."

"Of course, I mainly hear complaints. However, most are minor grievances. So far, our Wolf, Deer, and Water Plant Clans get along well. After being in exile for nearly ten sun cycles they are just happy to have a real home again. I have heard a rumor that some Duck Clan members in Monongahela Village are interested in moving here to be closer to distant relatives in Black Bear Village. We would be a little more independent with four clans, so I am hoping they do."

"I hope they wait until summer to make the move. But I hope they send warriors to help us clear fields so we can plant more of the three sisters. We will need the food reserves next winter."

"Spoken like a head matron! Is that what you want?" *I hope she says, "No." I am liking being head matron more than I thought I would.*

"When we were making that decision last summer, I said it did not matter to me if it was you or me. But after watching you at it for a few moons, now, I realize how well you are doing and know I am not ready yet. I am glad you accepted the position and just let me help you now and again. And with Tallow being elected as war chief, I just do not know how I could tell him what to do," Bright Star answered.

"I must admit, the duties have been more to my liking than expected."

"Good. We need not upset the council by changing head matrons for a while. Let us concentrate on having babies this winter."

"All right, but it would be nice to have Bright Moon here to share the burden."

"Well, she is gone. And she will be bringing her own child into the world soon. She will be busy enough."

———

THE WINTER SOLSTICE came and went. Winter continued with cold days and colder nights. Snow accumulated for days, then a warm up would result in melting followed by more snow in a seemingly endless cycle. About the time Water Mint noticed the days getting longer, she went into labor. By that time, Bright Star was advanced in her pregnancy and of little help to Water Mint.

Water Mint moved herself into the woman's lodge while Bright Star called on a couple of experienced midwives and their village shaman to ensure a safe and smooth birth. The experienced mother went through the labor with little pain. When the time was right, she used the rope attached to the lodge frame to pull herself up to a squatting position and pushed the baby onto a waiting deer hide. One attendant took the baby to clean her up, while a second helped Water Mint back onto the bed platform and cleaned her up.

When she was more comfortable, Bright Star was ready with some willow bark and mint tea. Water Mint then took her new daughter to her breast and let the perfect little child suckle.

"I will name her Fawn because she is so cute with those big eyes and long lashes. And her father will be thankful for the Deer Clan name. When she becomes a woman, maybe there will be a Water Plant Clan name for her," said Water Mint.

"I hope my delivery goes as easily as yours!" Bright Star exclaimed.

"The first one is usually the worst they tell me. But all three of mine have gone relatively smoothly," replied Water Mint.

———

The spring equinox was a few days away when Bright Star was awakened by a strong abdominal cramp.

"Another nightmare?" a sleepy Red Hand asked without opening his eyes.

"More than that, husband," she moaned. "I think it is my time. Help me get to the women's lodge."

A flurry of activity erupted in the Water Plant Clan longhouse. The sun was not up, but the whole clan was up and moving.

Water Mint started issuing orders like a war chief on a battlefield. "Red Hand, go to the Deer Clan longhouse and bring Marsh Hen back. She will be the head midwife for your wife. Tallow, take care of Fingerling and Dewdrop. I will take Fawn with me. Black Willow, carry some water skins to the women's lodge, get a fire started, and get some water heating up. Bright Star, when you have your next cramp, we will wait for it to stop, then move to the women's lodge." Everyone took their orders and proceeded to carry them out.

After many heartbeats, Bright Star felt another contraction beginning. When she moaned, Water Mint was at her side. When the contraction eased off, Water Mint, carrying Fawn at her breast for her morning feed, and Bright Star donned their thick winter moccasins and wrapped their elk hide winter blankets over their shoulders and started for the women's lodge.

Light gray smoke already billowed from the smoke hole, contrasting sharply with the still-black sky. But with the commotion, the village was beginning to awaken.

Bright Star and Water Mint entered the women's lodge to see preparations for the birth of Bright Star's first child underway. A bed was opened with soft deerskin blankets. A rope hung down from a support pole over the bed, water pots were warming by the fire pit, and fabric rags and towels were laid out by the bed.

Bright Star lay down in the bed and waited for the next contraction. After several nervous moments, another contraction started. But it eased before becoming as strong as the others. She began to worry about her baby. But the child began its regular movements within her belly.

A finger of time passed with no more pains.

"Why are there no more pains?" Bright Star asked Marsh Hen timidly.

"Sometimes the contractions start and stop. No one knows why. It just is. You may not feel another pain for days. One day soon the pains will come, and the child will be born. For now, you can go back to your lodge and make some more clothes or blankets for this little one," the older woman said.

Bright Star returned to her lodge slump-shouldered and depressed. *Bright Moon would have probably just pushed this baby right out and gone hunting. I do not know what to do.*

Red Hand asked, "What happened? I was ready to hold my little daughter, but she is still in your belly!"

"Not funny. The child is just not ready to make an appearance yet."

"We will be ready when she is." He put his arm around her and pulled her to his side to comfort her. She pushed him away and sat with a gloomy expression on her pretty face.

"There is little you can do to make a baby come when it is not ready. But your depression will certainly make the little one sad. Take up some stitching or something to keep you occupied," Water Mint offered.

Bright Star just laid down and cried herself to sleep. Red Hand felt guilty for trying to lighten the mood.

The morning of the equinox, Bright Star was up before the first gray of a new day spread across the overcast sky. She went to work making a big pot of corn gruel with dried blueberries and pieces of pecan nuts mixed in. She also went to the creek and brought back four deer stomach water bags full. There was a new stack of firewood next to the firepit and three days' worth of kindling ready for use. Every dish in the lodge was cleaned and stacked neatly and a big bag of mint and blackberry tea simmering.

"Glad you are feeling better. It is good to see you up and around," Red Hand complimented her as he dipped a ceramic cup into the tea bag.

"I feel great today!" as she went to their bed platform and started folding blankets. When she bent over to put the folded top elk skin blanket on the foot of the bed, she felt a gush of hot fluid splash down her inner thighs.

"What!" she shouted, then realized her water had broken.

Everyone in the longhouse jumped out of their beds and rushed to her.

"This is the real thing!" Water Mint smiled as she wrapped her arm around Bright Star. "Everyone, you know what to do. Red Hand, go fetch Marsh Hen. Tallow, get some wood and blankets set outside the women's lodge. Take Fingerling and Dewdrop with you. I'll take the baby. Black Willow, will you help me get this new mother to the women's lodge?"

"Of course, and this will be a longer day than our last trip!" Black Willow called from outside her bed chamber. Her husband, Hard Edge, joined Tallow.

The men spent the day trying to keep peace between Fingerling and Dewdrop, a never-ending task. Finally, they became tired enough to go to sleep late in the afternoon.

In the women's lodge, Bright Star was racked with painful contractions starting right after she was in her birthing bed, right after the sun turned the cold, overcast sky gray. As the morning progressed, the interval between contractions became shorter. The day passed from afternoon to evening without notice to the women coaching Bright Star through her first birthing experience.

"How long will this go on?" Bright Star asked, for about the tenth time since the pains started coming more frequently while increasing in intensity.

"Everyone is different, my child. But you are strong and holding up well. A couple more contractions and I will check your progress again," Marsh Hen replied.

Two contractions later, Marsh Hen slid two fingers into Bright Star's woman hole and reported,

"I can still only put two fingers on the baby's head. You still have a ways to go, child."

Bright Star started to say something when another strong contraction racked her body. "This is wearing me out," the young woman said to no one as the contraction eased.

"Try to keep your breathing controlled during the pains. It makes it harder when you hold your breath," Marsh Hen reprimanded.

Bright Star concentrated on breathing evenly through the next contraction. It seemed to help.

Marsh Hen checked again and reported that some progress had occurred. "You are doing well, young woman, keep up the good work," she complimented Bright Star.

Well after the sun had gone down, the old midwife asked Bright Moon if she was ready to push.

"I think I can," the soon-to-be mother huffed.

With Bright Star holding herself up in a squatting position, her hand on the baby's head, Marsh Hen said, "Not yet...not yet...not yet. Now, push with all you have!"

Bright Star pushed, and nothing happened. She caught her breath again as Water Mint wiped the sweat from her face while helping her maintain balance, she pushed again. Pain seared her woman parts as what felt like an oak log passed between her legs, and a great relief washed over her.

Marsh Hen expertly guided the child onto a clean deer hide, took a length of thick sinew, tied off the umbilical cord in two places, then severed it between the ties, and took the squalling baby to a bench to clean the newborn boy.

Water Mint kept Bright Star in her squatting position until she expelled the afterbirth onto a special fawn skin that Bright Star would bury in a chosen location outside the longhouse. Red Hand would not be allowed to help her in that chore.

When Marsh Hen was cleaning the baby up, she made the discovery that the boy had a deformed foot. His right foot was normal, but his left was sort of round with short bones and one ankle bone that stuck out at an odd angle. He would have a noticeable limp and trouble running.

"Bright Star, you need to prepare yourself. This little human is not completely normal," Marsh Hen said in a subdued and serious manner.

"What is it?" came the young mother's panicked response.

"See for yourself. He has a club foot and an unusual bone. We could save you and him a lot of trouble by taking him into the forest and letting the earth reclaim him," the old woman replied somberly as she held the baby up, awkwardly showing Bright Star the deformed foot. The baby was practically screaming in his discomfort.

"Give me that child!" Bright Star screamed. She took the baby, who was not entirely cleaned yet and held him to her breast. He eagerly suckled as he calmed down. "There will be no talk of exposing this child!" She looked at Marsh Hen with daggers in her eyes.

"Just trying to save you trouble in the days ahead, child. Do not get angry with me for trying to shield you, and him, from a lifetime of grief. You know the other children will tease him mercilessly for a simple mistake of nature," the old woman replied defensively.

"Thank you for caring, but this child is destined for greatness, I can feel it. Some of nature's greatest wonders are not symmetrical. I will hear no more about it." She looked lovingly at her baby. *You will always be special in my eyes, even with your bad foot, my son.* Bright Star named the child Bone for the unusual bone that protruded from his ankle.

CHAPTER 2

BABY BONE

Thirty canoes slid into the landing at River Birch Village from New Long Pine Village on the day before the Solstice Celebration was to begin. As late arrivals, their campsite was relegated to the edge of a bog where mosquitoes would be a problem. Cedar smoke would wash across their temporary home for the entire time they were in camp.

The first act was to set piles of cedar branches around the perimeter of their camp and ignite the ones that the wind would carry the acrid smoke through the campground to drive the annoying pests away. By surrounding their campsite with piles of cedar branches, they could keep the biting insects at bay no matter which direction the wind was blowing.

Once the camp was set up, most of the women set about making fire rings, including a large one in the center of their ring of tentlike temporary lodges. Once the firepits were established, bags of gruel, various stews and teas, strips of deer meat, grouse, and turkey, and fish were prepared.

Water Mint and Tallow, along with Bright Star and Red Hand, and their babies, walked over to the Deer Clan longhouse where they sat under a ramada along with the head matrons and war chiefs of all the Monongahela villages.

The new arrivals were given cups of sassafras and mint tea and sweet corn cakes. The New Long Pine babies were big hits with all the matrons and were passed from one to another until all had met the youngsters. Water Mint's daughter Fawn had now seen five moons, and Bright Star's son, Bone, had seen three moons. Fawn was able to squirm and roll over while Bone was completely at the mercy of whoever was holding him. At his young age, Bone's club foot was hidden in his swaddling blanket. It would be his walking and running that would be affected as he grew older.

Corn Stalk held Bone up and said, "Just look at those intelligent eyes!"

Traveler, sitting to his wife's right side, said, "Yes, he is a born leader."

Immediately, Bone swiveled his head to Traveler. The baby stared at the aging trader with wide open eyes and a big smile. He tried to lunge toward the elder and reached a shaking arm out in that direction.

"I think he wants you to hold him, Traveler," said Bright Star from ten paces away on the outside of the circle of matrons and their escorts.

Corn Stalk handed the baby over to her husband. Traveler cradled the tiny boy and said, "My, you are a handsome little warrior."

Bone's reaction to Traveler had everyone under the ramada gasping in awe. The child shook like he was having a convulsion but laughed hysterically. He arched his back like he wanted to be closer to the man who was holding him and looked at Traveler with unblinking concentration. No one had ever seen such a young baby react to anyone other than its mother in such a manner.

"Talk to him some more, Traveler," Bright Star said.

"My heart sings to meet such a dedicated fan," Traveler said while giving the boy a wide smile.

Bone's features lit up, showcasing his own wide smile followed by a loud laugh.

"This is a first," Bright Star quipped.

Traveler noted a very jealous look in his wife's eyes.

"We will talk again, young warrior." Traveler talked to Bone like he was a grown man, then passed him back to Corn Stalk.

"Oh, I do look forward to spoiling the little ones!" Corn Stalk spoke to everyone under the ramada. Bone started to fuss, and Bright Star stepped in and took up her child. About that time, Fawn made the rounds to Corn Stalk, and the Head Matron was rewarded with a very loving little girl.

Bright Star decided Bone had had enough excitement for one day and started to leave the crowded ramada. Bone craned his little neck trying to see Traveler.

"Come, little one, I think it is time for your nap." Bright Star hurried to the New Long Pine Village campsite, changed the wet moss absorbent, put fresh moss in the mesh holder, and wrapped a new loin cloth around the baby's tiny bottom. Finally, she sat with her back against a basket and held Bone up to her breast. At first, he was disinterested, still craning his neck around like he was searching for something or someone. After a bit of struggling, he gave up, started suckling, and fell sound asleep, Bright Star's nipple still half in his mouth.

A short while later, a bedraggled looking Red Hand came into their tent, followed by a boisterous Fingerling and Dewdrop.

"Can I trade places with him?" Red Hand tipped his head toward Bone. Fingerling got a sour look on his face, and Dewdrop just looked on with her mouth open wide. "These two have worn me out more than a battle against ten-tens of Haudenosaunee warriors." Red Hand winked at Fingerling and Dewdrop, then gave Bright Star a pleading look.

"Where is Tallow?" Bright Star changed the subject while she laid Bone down on a sleeping pallet and closed her shirt to cover her exposed breast.

"Said he was going over to the ramada to escort Water Mint and Fawn back to our campsite. Red Hand sat down where Bright Star had been nursing Bone. Just when he leaned back to rest, Fingerling and Dewdrop started climbing on him.

"Do you two never rest?" Red Hand asked the two older children.

"Never!" replied Fingerling.

"Sometimes, if I get tired," answered Dewdrop.

Bright Star looked at Dewdrop and said, "Come and tell me what you have been doing to get Red Hand so tired."

The young girl slid off Red Hand, leaving Fingerling wrestling with their older cousin, and climbed into Bright Star's arms where she sat a couple paces from Red Hand.

"First we walked down by the river. We saw... lots...of...c..." And Dewdrop was sound asleep.

A short time later, the three children and Red Hand were sleeping peacefully on bed pallets, and Bright Star was at the central firepit talking with some of the other women. There were a few from New Long Pine Village, though most had wandered over to the Monongahela Village campsite to catch up with friends they had not seen since the wedding of Corn Stalk and Traveler the previous autumn. Others from various camps came to see how the new village was fairing.

A very happy Beebalm came up to Bright Star. "Sorry you were not able to make the trip when Red

Oak returned from the Lenape lands. Not sure if you heard, but Bright Moon did deliver her baby in Sun Town. He is a very healthy boy with yellow hair and blue eyes. His name is Acorn, but Yellow Hair confided in Red Oak that the boy's name would be *Erik* when they reached his Norse people. By the time they went upriver, he was already holding his head up and rolling over. And Red Oak said Bright Moon was amazing. Two days after delivering her son, she was pounding corn and hoeing in the crop fields."

"I would expect nothing less of her. Except she would never pound corn or hoe weeds when she lived with us. She must be growing up! I have not had a chance to talk about these things since we arrived here. My heart sings, thank you for bringing this news."

"You have not yet heard about the battle they were in?" Beebalm asked.

"What battle?" a suddenly worried Bright Star asked.

"Oh! Sorry, Red Oak can give you better details—he was there. But she was not hurt. According to my husband, thanks to Yellow Hair's plan, none of their party was so much as scratched. Red Oak says Yellow Hair's plan was brilliant, and they carried it out perfectly."

"You had me worried for a moment, and then you made me happy. Thank you for bringing me this news."

"I will make sure Red Oak finds you and gives you

a full report before you return to your village. And the other news is after his return, the Creator has placed a little one in my womb!"

"That is particularly good news. Corn Stalk must be ecstatic about that!" Bright Star embraced her distant cousin-in-law.

"She is. And I should probably get back now. The men will be hungry soon."

"Yes, we have two deer roasts to prepare tonight. I look forward to chatting some more." Bright Star gave Beebalm another hug and went to put more wood on the fire. She was now highly anticipating her talk with Red Oak.

That night, when all was quiet, and they were in the blankets of their own sleeping pallet, Bright Star said to Red Hand, "You should have seen the way Bone reacted to Traveler today. No one had ever seen anything like it. His little body quivered he was so excited to be in the elder's arms. And the way he reacted when Traveler talked to him. I wish I could get that kind of response. He laughed and smiled from ear to ear, but never took his eyes off the man. It was unbelievable!"

"Yes. It is the main topic on every tongue. Our three moons son is already a legend!"

"What should we do? I mean, is it healthy for a baby to act like that?"

"I think no one knows the answer to that question—it seems nothing like it has ever happened. My guess is there was something in Traveler's voice. Maybe only Bone's tiny ears could hear it."

———

BY THE TIME Bone started crawling, his club foot was noticeable, but it did not slow him down in the least. He could get around like any other baby his age. Fawn was already taking her first tentative steps when she had seen only eight moons, but Bone could, and did, cover more ground than her. Bone's crawling started when he had seen five moons.

Corn Stalk and Traveler made it to New Long Pine Village for their Green Corn Celebration

After the elders arrived and sat down along the central firepit of the Water Plant Clan longhouse, Traveler told Water Mint that she was doing a great job organizing New Long Pine Village. Bone, snuggled to his mother's chest suckling, stopped and looked to where Traveler was seated. Bone rolled out of his mother's arms and began slithering like a snake around the firepit toward Traveler. Apparently, he thought he was not moving fast enough because he got up on his hands and knees, like some child a moon older than him would, and crawled straight to Traveler, and climbed into the elder's lap with a wide grin on his face.

"So, you remember me, huh?" Traveler said to the boy. Bone giggled and reached for Traveler's face.

CHAPTER 3

GROWING

By the time Bone had seen two sun cycles, his mother was preparing to give birth to her second child. Bone was now walking and increasing his limited vocabulary almost daily. He had no idea he was walking with a limp, and it certainly did not slow him down. Constant vigilance was required to keep him inside the longhouse during the cold winter moons. Fortunately for Bright Star, she had her cousins, Fingerling and Dewdrop, around to lend her a hand.

When Bright Star went into labor in the middle of the Awakening Moon, the supervision of the toddler fell on his older cousins, who dutifully carried out their task, but not without complaining. Red Hand made sure Fingerling and Dewdrop were well rewarded for their effort.

Bright Star's labor was uneventful, and she delivered a little girl with a head full of raven-black hair.

The little one's eyes were dark and very large, like looking at a full moon rising over the treetops. Bright Star had always planned to name her first daughter Bright Moon, after her sister who had followed her man to a distant land across the ocean. Bright Star had no idea how much like that namesake her daughter would become.

Bone treated the baby like a curiosity but soon lost interest in the little creature that just laid around sleeping or crying. He was a little upset that the baby got to suckle his mother's teat whenever it wanted to, causing him to wait sometimes. He soon learned to fill his cravings with normal food and gradually lost interest in his mother's milk.

By the time he had seen four sun cycles, he realized he was a brother and became protective of his little sister, who was getting around fine on her own unsteady little legs. He saw it as his duty to keep her out of the firepit and inside the longhouse when the weather was cold or stormy.

He was becoming more curious about the world outside his lodge and explored everything he could. He usually dragged Bright Moon along with him. One day, as they went making their way around the outside of the longhouse, things got a little interesting. Dewdrop was intently busy watching Fingerling and a couple other boys playing hoop 'n stick and lost track of where Bone was leading Bright Moon.

Passing by the smelly pit, Bright Moon lost her balance and started to topple into the latrine. Bone happened to look back and saw her start to fall. He acted quickly and caught her bare feet just as she went over the edge. He was not able to prevent her hands and head from dipping into the foul ooze in the pit. After dragging her out, he grabbed her upper arm and dragged her to the big mortar where Bright Star was pounding some of the previous summer's corn kernels with a log pestle.

Bright Moon was screaming and had managed to smear the refuse on her hands across Bone's torso by the time they reached their mother. Bright Star looked at her children aghast. When she looked over at Water Mint, who was talking to another woman, she could see the Head Matron trying not to laugh. A spontaneous belly laugh from the circle of women broke out as both children screamed for attention.

Fingerling and Dewdrop came running to the commotion and stopped in their tracks. Fingerling saw the mothers laughing and laughed himself, not really sure what was so funny. By now, his cousins were smeared with refuse from the latrine pit and smelled like it. He and Dewdrop backed away, him chuckling and her crying.

Bright Star and Water Mint led the two smelly children to the creek and washed them from head to toe. Since both were totally naked, no clothing needed to be washed. Later, when Bone went to take Moon for another exploratory hike, she refused to go with him.

Bone's most notable trait was his adulation of

the elder, Traveler. Everyone marveled at how the child, at four sun cycles, hung on every word the elder spoke. The fact that Bone was only in contact with Traveler about six times in a sun cycle made it quite remarkable.

"He seems to think you are some great spirit," Corn Stalk said when she and Traveler were in their sleeping skins after a visit from the New Long Pine villagers.

"I have not been able to conjure what he sees in me," Traveler replied. "Are you jealous that he gives me so much attention?"

"Of course I am! I am the Head Matron around here. You are just my husband. Head Matrons always want all the attention, especially from their grandchildren. It is a good thing Moon finds me more attractive than you, or you would find your belongings outside my lodge." Corn Stalk had a hard time keeping the mirth from her voice as she commented.

He squeezed her hand and said, "Yes, I guess I am lucky for that!"

Whenever Traveler and Bone were in the same village, Traveler had a constant companion. Bone would follow the elder everywhere he went. When Traveler sat down to rest, Bone crawled into his lap and snuggled. No one had ever seen anything like it.

"Still, I worry about him," Corn Stalk would say. "So far, that club foot has not slowed Bone down, nor have the other small children started teasing him about it. They will, I am afraid, when he gets a little older."

"The people in your lineage have great strength of character. I suspect Bone will not be an exception. I think he will adapt and get along well. However, I do not think he is destined to be a great warrior. That foot will slow him too much in battle. We will see what the spirits have in mind for him. Has Bright Star said anything about Wolf contacting her, or however he used to communicate with Bright Moon?"

"No. She has not mentioned anything to me. And I think she would. I worry about his future," Corn Stalk lamented.

"You worry about everyone's future. Maybe you should let the future take care of itself."

"A good strategy for a trader, perhaps. But a head matron cannot afford such a lazy approach to life. Otherwise, her people would not last a generation."

"You are right, of course. I should keep my rogue thoughts to myself!"

"Traveler, if you kept your rogue thoughts quiet, my life would become so boring, I would put myself in a canoe and float away to the lands of the Illini People for some excitement! Your tongue keeps me on my toes. And I love you for that."

The elders brought their lips together for a passionate kiss.

———

THREE SUN CYCLES LATER, Bone had a sister and a girl cousin following him everywhere he went. He treated his club foot like it was a normal appendage, not letting it slow him down in the slightest. That odd bone, for which he was named, that stuck out from his foot was a nuisance, but he ignored it the best he could. It was a challenge for his mother to make moccasins that protected that bone while covering his odd-shaped foot. The special moccasin was difficult, sometimes painful, to put on and take off.

He continued to dote on the girls, but his preference was to go with his father. Red Hand was now taking him hunting for grouse, rabbits, and other small animals. He was shooting a child's bow and trying to use a bola.

Older children, indeed, were beginning to tease him about his foot. He did his best to ignore their taunts. One day a boy a sun cycle older than Bone got him running, then spun around and tripped him just to get a laugh from his friends. When Bone laughed with them, the boy gave up teasing Bone.

As time went by, Bone's admiration for Traveler grew. Whenever he could get to Traveler, he bombarded the elder with questions about where he had been and the things he had seen. It turned out to be therapy for Traveler's aching joints and muscles. Relating past adventures did more than take the elder's mind off his pains and stiffness. Telling and retelling the stories also improved his memory. In a way, he wished the boy had come into his life at a younger age so that he could have taken him on some of those trading expeditions to faraway places.

———

"YOU ARE nothing but a coward and sissy, always dragging your sister and cousin everywhere you go. Of course, that is because you cannot do warrior things with that stupid club foot slowing you down. I bet you wish you were never born. Or is it you wish you were born a girl? Then you could play with corn husk dolls like you want to," chided Little Hawk, a boy in the Deer Clan who had seen ten summers, just like Bone.

"You have no call to say such things, and it makes you less a warrior than me," Bone replied.

That was just the reaction Little Hawk was looking for. He balled his fists and charged into Bone thinking he could overpower him and make him look weak and helpless in front of the older boys. Bone lost his balance and fell into the dusty plaza, but he was far from finished. He dragged Little Hawk down with him, and soon the boys were rolling in the dirt punching, gouging, and kicking.

Finally, Bone got a clean punch into Little Hawk's jaw, snapping his adversary's mouth shut, loosening a couple teeth while slicing off the tip of the boy's tongue that was between his teeth. The fight ended with Little Hawk's tongue bleeding profusely and him crying out in pain.

Bone tried to stand but discovered he could not put weight on his deformed foot. The small bone that protruded from his foot, that had given him his name, lay flat against his misshapen foot and was bleeding from a slit in the skin at the base of that odd bone.

Adults quickly came to the scene of the commotion and started calling for a healer. Two burly warriors grabbed the boys by the shoulders and dragged them apart. Water Mint and Bright Star soon arrived.

Water Mint quickly assessed the situation and asked the child witnesses what happened. She could tell Little Hawk could not talk with his injured tongue, and now Bone was writhing in pain with his clubbed foot covered in blood. The children all said that Little Hawk started it by calling Bone a weak sissy.

Bright Star was trying to calm Bone and had his foot elevated, wiping blood away with a piece of tanned deer skin when Red Hand arrived.

"What happened here?" he demanded.

Bright Star explained what she knew. Red Hand picked Bone up and started for the Water Plant Clan longhouse, keeping the boy's foot higher than his heart.

"He needs Willow Bark to look at his foot, Red Hand. She needs to get Little Hawk's bleeding stopped first, then she will tend to Bone," Bright Star told Red Hand.

"She can come to the Water Plant longhouse when she is finished with Little Hawk," Red Hand replied.

"No. Take him to my lodge," Willow Bark told Red Hand, leaving no room for argument. She had Little Hawk on his feet with a piece of soft deer skin in his mouth to staunch the bleeding. "Come with me," she told the boy as she guided him across the plaza to her small lodge.

Willow Bark's lodge was a downsized version of the larger longhouses. It was oval shaped with the entrance on the east side. A frame of saplings with the butt end stuck in the ground in an oval pattern, then bent and lashed together formed the overall domed shape standing about two times the height of a tall warrior. Cross ties of smaller saplings strength-ened the structure. A bark covering protected the interior, keeping it dry and warm inside. And addi-tional framework of smaller saplings was lashed to the outside to keep the bark walls tied down and add strength. This smaller lodge had two smoke holes in the roof to allow smoke to leave the building. Those smoke holes could be closed in bad weather. The east facing door opening was sealed with an elk hide door hanging that was doubled in winter.

The interior was one large room with a central firepit running lengthwise along the floor. A frame-work along the south wall provided bed platforms for a few people. In this case, Willow Bark was the only permanent resident, but she had bed space for a few patients. Under the bed platforms and above them were storage places for blankets, clothing, ceremonial objects, and other belongings. She was the village healer, and the rest of the lodge was a virtual apothecary with racks of drying medicinal and food plants. Around the firepit were various metates with grinding stones for preparing medicines and poultices for wounds and other injuries.

Willow Bark escorted Little Hawk and his mother into the lodge and directed them to one of the bed platforms. Red Hand, carrying Bone, and Bright Star following were directed to another platform. Bright Star rolled a sleeping skin and propped Bone's injured foot up on it.

Bone's pain had subsided to a dull ache, and he was no longer sobbing by the time Willow Bark came back to him. When he first came in he was given a tea containing powdered black willow and slippery elm bark for the pain. He was resting quietly, but not sleeping. Bright Star had gone to the council meeting to determine if either boy would be punished in any way for the fight. It was finally decided that boys will be boys and fights will occur. Sometimes one or both get hurt. Nothing new or anything to be concerned about.

Willow Bark examined Bone's foot and decided the odd bone was irreparably broken. No ligaments were attached to it—it was just a freak bone that was only attached on one end. It may have been intended as one of the foot bones that were entwined in the mass of his clubbed foot, but somehow grew separately and was just there. She decided to cut the skin around it and use the excess skin to sew over the hole where the bone had been attached to top of his foot. A poultice was put in place to ensure it would not be invaded by evil spirits.

She determined that when the boys were wrestling around on the ground, the bone was broken off. She said that Bone was probably lucky it happened when he was still growing. The bone would be more of a problem as he grew older if it was still in place. Red Hand agreed with her diagnosis and treatment. The wound would be painful for many days to come but would heal better than if they tried to reattach the abnormal bone.

Willow Bark wrapped the bone in a rabbit skin and gave it to Bone to do with as he wished. He took it, and Red Hand carried him back to the Water Plant Clan longhouse. They arrived as the council meeting was ending. When the other matrons left, Bright Star asked Bone how he was feeling. He said it hurt a lot, but he felt strange with part of his foot gone. Then, he offered to show her the bone in the rabbit skin.

Deciding it meant something to him, she reached out for it. He handed it over, and she unwrapped it. It was still red colored from the blood that had soaked into it.

"I think you have a new name, Bone. I think I will

know you as 'Redbone' from now on," said his mother.

"Redbone it is!" echoed Red Hand.

"I am Redbone," the boy agreed, as he took the half-finger-length bone back from his mother. "Redbone will start his spirit bundle, and this will be the first treasure in it."

"I cannot think of a better place for it, my son," said Bright Star.

"Your first step into manhood," Red Hand chimed in.

"When will I be a woman?" Bright Moon, now eight summers, asked.

"All too soon!" Bright Star and Red Hand replied.

After the incident in the plaza earlier in the day, Bright Moon had decided she would become Redbone's personal spirit helper. She could already run faster and handle most weapons better than any ten-sun-cycles boys in the village. It would not take her long to learn to fight better. She envisioned becoming the warrior her aunt she was named after had been before she left for her husband's homeland.

CHAPTER 4

BLUE DEER

Time passed quickly, and by the time Redbone had seen ten and four sun cycles, changes were taking place in New Long Pine Village and the Monongahela nation. Six long-houses now stood in the plaza. In addition, there were eight single-family dwellings, six clan women's lodges, a warrior society lodge, ten sweat lodges, a healer's lodge, and two wedding lodges.

The responsibilities and duties of Head Matron were wearing on Water Mint.

"Bright Star, with two children growing so fast, a son already an adult warrior, and a daughter who has entered the women's lodge, I just do not think I can keep up anymore," Water Mint lamented to her niece.

"Trust me, I hear what you are saying. Are you saying you wish to step down as Head Matron?" Bright Star asked.

"You know my thoughts. I need not even speak aloud for you to get my meaning."

"Would it be possible for you and me to switch roles? I will take over the village Head Matron duties, and you assume my place as Water Plant Clan Head Matron. Would that be acceptable to you?"

"Only you could devise such a perfect solution. I would still have some duties, but you could take over the bigger things. I like the idea."

"I will be calling on your experience and wisdom more often than you imagine, but the plan is agreeable to me," said Bright Star.

"We just need to convince the Council," added Water Mint.

"I think if we present it together, we can make it happen. The Green Corn Celebration would be the perfect time for the ceremony."

"I know Tallow will welcome the idea. What about Red Hand?"

"Oh, I am sure he will be agreeable. I think he has some ideas about the war chief role," Bright Moon replied.

"Good! Tallow thinks he is getting too old to deal with the youngest warriors. And now we have many more than when we first started," Water Mint said.

"In fact, Red Hand left this morning for Black Bear Village. He has some ideas about strengthening the defenses of our northern territory. Those northern Haudenosaunee are getting braver again." Bright Star was becoming concerned that their fighting was far from over, and her son would never be a warrior to help defend their homelands.

"Did he talk about this with Tallow?"

"I saw them talking at the central firepit this morning. It looked like Tallow gave him a pat on the back as Red Hand and his party started for the palisade opening."

"I just wanted to make sure they are of the same mind. But I would prefer such actions go through the Council, if you see what I mean."

"Of course. I think Red Hand is on a scouting mission and will bring his findings before the Council before any action is taken."

"I think this is a good way to look at the problem. Thank you for telling me."

"I will still discuss everything with you if the Council votes to make me Head Matron of the village, as you discuss all of it with me, now," said Bright Star.

———

"Mother, Fast Hawk and I are planning to take a canoe to Monongahela Village. I have not seen Traveler since Grandmother Corn Stalk stepped down as Head Matron at the Solstice Celebration." Redbone did not need to voice his concern that his idol was growing feeble and would walk the Path of the Ancestors all too soon.

"Could you wait until Red Hand returns from

Black Bear Village. It should only delay you ten days. I like to have a man in our chamber each night," Bright Star replied.

Redbone knew there was no danger concerning their chamber, but Bright Moon was becoming difficult for their mother to deal with. The ten-and-two summers girl was demanding she become a warrior while Bright Star wanted her to be a clan maid. Arguments ensued nearly every evening, often resulting in Bright Moon stomping out of the longhouse and spending the night out in the forest somewhere. When Red Hand or Redbone were around, they could quiet the arguments and sooth the parties' heated tempers.

"I will wait no more than ten days," Redbone replied.

For the next ten days, Redbone packed a few tanned hides that he had collected. He had ten deer, two elk, five beaver, one wolverine, two fisher, and five raccoon skins, well-tanned with the fur on. He also had five tens of arrows with chert points, choke cherry shafts, and grouse feather fletching, along with otter skin quivers. His sister, Bright Moon, had made the arrow points—she was better at chipping stone than he was.

Red Hand returned with a great surprise for Redbone. When he had gotten to Black Bear Village, he found out that their warriors had recently repelled a band Haudenosaunee raiders. In the process the Black Bear warriors had captured two of the enemy's bark canoes. The crafts were well built with curved ends that would repel splashing in rough water. Red Hand knew that Redbone dreamed of being a trader because his deformed foot greatly handicapped him in a fight, so a warrior's life was out of the question for the young man. Red Hand also knew that his son idolized the former trader named Traveler. Traveler always talked the virtues of bark canoes because they were lighter than the typical dugouts.

When Red Hand presented the bark canoe to Redbone, his eyes filled with tears.

"Father, I know not what to say. It is what I have dreamed about. How can I ever repay your kindness?"

"You just did, my son." Redbone bearhugged his father and openly wept on his shoulder.

During that interaction, thunderers announced their approach from the southwest. In a hand of time, rain was pounding on the overturned craft along the bank at the canoe landing. It rained for several hands of time before slowing to a drizzle, causing Redbone and Fast Hawk to delay their trip to Monongahela Village for a day.

As they were preparing to depart, Bright Star asked, "Are you sure you can handle this boat in the high water? In a day or two it will be down to normal flow."

"Yes, mother, we can paddle a canoe in high water," Redbone replied.

Bright Moon and Red Hand looked at each other and rolled their eyes. They were comfortable with the young men's ability to navigate the river—it was only a little higher than normal already. She wished that she had been invited on the trip. She loved an adventure as much as anyone, and she always enjoyed seeing relatives in Monongahela Village. On top of that, she figured being close to Fast Hawk for several days and nights would not be distasteful in the least, even though she had not gone to the women's lodge yet. In her fringed buckskin hunting shirt, leggings, and dark-tanned breechclout, and with loose black hair, she looked anything but an available young maiden.

Right after they shoved off, Redbone and Fast Hawk found that the bark canoe handled differently than a dugout. It rode higher in the water and did not just plow through the current. It was affected by every eddy and cross-current the river threw at them. But they soon learned the nuances and had the craft going the way they intended. By the time they had negotiated four major turns, they were feeling very confident in Redbone's new canoe. Before they left New Long Pine Village, he had painted white hands on each side of the bow to signal to anyone they encountered that it was a trader's canoe. He also carried a straight, white shaft with three white feathers attached that would identify him as a trader.

After their first night on the river, they set out in

the morning before the sun topped the hills to the east. The shadows cast by the high hills made the river more difficult to read. When they reached a rocky stretch right after a large creek entered the flow, pushing them farther west, Fast Hawk missed a large rock below the surface. When the current pushed them up and over the rock, the canoe wobbled, then struck the obstacle just before they were past it.

The unexpected jar caused Redbone to drop his paddle. Before he could retrieve it from the fast current, the canoe turned in the eddy and swung them around, so they were moving backward downriver. Though Redbone could not reach his paddle, he had forethought to tie a lanyard to the handle and reeled it in quickly. By then, they were out of control and moving in a twisting pattern at the whim of the rushing current.

As they were carried downriver, they were in a desperate struggle to get the boat under control. Dragged into the choppier water, they were soon taking on water from all directions. An occasional collision with a submerged rock or tree limb added to their predicament.

Just when it looked as though they were about to swamp, they entered a large, quiet pool and regained control.

"That was too close!" they both shouted in unison.

"I see a large gravel bar to the east side of the river," Fast Hawk declared.

"Paddle for it. We need to get this water out of the canoe quickly!" Redbone declared.

They found a deep, fast-moving current right along the gravel bar. It required them to make it to the end of the bar, then turn to the inside passage to get to a place where they could safely land. That took extra effort because the canoe, heavy with water floated past the gravel bar. They had to turn the sluggish boat around and backtrack upstream many paces to make it to safety. After that struggle, they needed to rest before unloading their packs and lugging them to the dry gravel in the middle of the gravel bar. Adding to their workload, silt had settled at the downstream end of the gravel bar, and they had to slog through that to get their gear to dry ground.

Once empty, the canoe was easy enough to tip over and dump the water out. That done, it was easy enough to carry to the dry, warm gravel in full sunlight. They soon had their wet clothing and gear spread out on the gravel drying. Redbone learned he had done a good job wrapping his trade goods and none got wet. But the skins they were wrapped in needed to dry. All afternoon they laid around eating and drinking while their clothing and gear dried.

When a shadow from a tall tree on the west side of the river fell across their resting place, they decided they had better pack up and get to a better campsite before dark.

"We learned a lot today," Fast Hawk declared.

"I hope!" replied Redbone.

Three days later, the confluence of the Kiskiminetus River came into view. Redbone knew the campsite on the north bank of that river was where they would stop for the night. They would be in Monongahela Village before the following midday.

A small contingent of warriors met them at the canoe landing outside Monongahela Village.

"Welcome, cousin!" a burly warrior named Strong Elk spoke to Redbone.

Redbone smiled and said, "Greetings, cousin!" to the big warrior once known as Sprout. "How is it in Monongahela Village?"

"All is well here. I see you managed to steal a bark canoe. It looks like a good one. Haudenosaunee made, if my reasoning is correct."

"Sort of stolen, I guess. Father went to Black Bear Village. They had defeated a raiding party and captured two of these canoes. Red Hand brought one to me as a present. I think the warriors who paddled down the Ohi-yo had no more use for it."

"Yes, hard to walk the Path of the Ancestors in a canoe. My heart sings for you. Looks like you have it full of trade goods. Do you plan to make us poor?"

"If I can. How is Traveler?" Redbone could no longer contain his curiosity.

"You will have to ask him. All he likes to do is sit

and talk. I think his wandering days are over. And Grandmother is content to sit all day with him," Strong Elk replied.

"You men, carry these trader bags and baskets to the Corn Clan longhouse."

"Are you a war leader now?"

"I think Grandmother has told Red Oak to over-look my faults," the warrior replied.

Redbone and Strong Elk laughed while the others tentatively smiled. It would not be good to openly laugh at the Head Matron or War Chief's expense, whether they understood the joke or not.

Redbone also noted a large trader's canoe in the long line of overturned craft along the canoe landing. The long dugout had a white lance with three white feathers painted on the bow.

It seems I have heard that canoe described somewhere in the past. He hoped to get an answer soon.

Strong Elk led Redbone and Fast Hawk to the Corn Clan longhouse. It was a bit cool for the season, and Redbone noted dark gray smoke billowing from all three smoke holes along the roofline of the largest longhouse in Monongahela Village.

"They must be preparing a feast for us!" said Redbone as he turned and winked at Fast Hawk.

"I think it is for the trader, Blue Deer. He is here from Lenape Town. Last I saw, he and Traveler were trading stories and laughing often."

A twinge of jealousy unexpectedly struck

Redbone. He wanted Traveler's undivided attention. He kept his feelings to himself.

They slipped through the elk skin door hanging and entered the large room. The air was heavy with woodsmoke from the central firepit and tobacco from the several pipes that individuals were puffing on.

Traveler noticed the newcomers immediately and waved them over to his place near the head of the elongated firepit.

"Come join us, Redbone and Little Hawk." Traveler was unaware that Fast Hawk had been through the rituals and was now a man.

"It is Fast Hawk, now, Grandfather," Redbone corrected.

"Cause for celebration!" Traveler quickly added, then proceeded to introduce Blue Deer, Water Racer, Blue Deer's apprentice, Redbone, and Fast Hawk. Everyone else in the room knew each other.

Redbone noted that Red Oak was present. The war chief nodded to Strong Elk, who promptly left the gathering. Redbone knew Strong Elk was on patrol and needed to get back to his duties. He also noted that Corn Stalk was not at her customary place beside Traveler. This gathering was all men.

Two young women soon brought a bowl of corn stew and acorn cakes to the new guests and gathered the empty bowls from the rest of the group. They carried the stacks of bowls through the door hanging into another section of the longhouse.

"Blue Deer has been telling us some of his exploits from the Great Crab Bay and up the Lenape River. What brings you young men to our council?" Traveler asked.

Obviously embarrassed to be in such a gathering of older men, Redbone studied the mat weave at his feet for several heartbeats. Finally, he quietly said, "Redbone wished to show you his new canoe and has a few trade goods to barter with. Fast Hawk came to help me maneuver the new canoe."

"Did you hollow the log yourself? You have been busy since I last saw you."

"No, Grandfather. Red Hand went to Black Bear Village for a war council. Some Haudenosaunee warriors had come downriver to test the Black Bear defenses. That was their mistake. The Black Bear warriors captured two of the enemy canoes. Somehow Red Hand became the owner of one, and he brought it to me because he knew I wanted a bark canoe."

"You have a bark canoe? Is it in good condition?"

"Yes, it is practically new. I painted it with new birch oil like you said is wise, then painted a white hand on each side of the bow."

"Sounds like you are taking great care of it," Traveler complimented the young man.

"Sorry to interrupt your council. We will go do something else," Redbone said.

"We were just telling stories. Have a seat and

listen awhile—you might learn something," Traveler replied.

Redbone and Fast Hawk moved to the outer circle of older men and took a seat on the woven floor mat.

Most men in the room sat quietly while Blue Deer or Traveler told one tale or another about trading, enduring storms, and narrow escapes from hostile situations. Two of the highlights involved Redbone's aunt, Bright Moon, and uncle, Yellow Hair. The more Redbone heard of those two, the more he wished he could find them if they were never coming back.

Blue Deer narrated, "Long Cat and Blue Deer had left them below the pass that would take them from the Lenape River to the Great River. The trader Broken Bow made his way to Round Track Village in the Lenape lands a sun cycle later where he had reported the couple and their small child had sailed on the great canoe of the Norse people and were never seen again. He reported the next time we saw him that the great canoe came back, but Bull Moose and his Micmac people burned their boat before the Norse ever had a chance to get away. They all died, but there was no woman aboard. No Norse ever returned to Bull Moose Village."

"Nobody knows what happened to Bright Moon and Yellow Hair, then?" Redbone bravely asked.

"No. They just sailed away. No other news has come forth."

"It is a shame. Yellow Hair told me about some of

the marvelous things the Norse know how to do, and the things they make are like magic to us. Someday, maybe they will return to our shores." Traveler spoke with great remorse in his voice as he shook his head.

As the afternoon wore on, the men in the room began to leave. First, one would leave, then another. Finally, Red Oak stood and declared, "It is time to get something accomplished for this day. Let us leave these traders to their business." With that, everyone except Redbone, Fast Hawk, Blue Deer, Water Racer, and Traveler stood and left the longhouse. Redbone, Fast Hawk, and Water Racer stood in deference to the older men as they left.

"Shall we walk down to the landing and look at Redbone's new canoe?" Traveler asked.

Redbone thought his heart would pound right out of his chest. *Traveler wants to see my canoe!* He jumped to his feet and waited while the others slowly stood. Blue Deer helped Traveler stand. He had been sitting so long, his old bones and joints were stiff. Redbone saw Traveler's walking stick laying on the mat and quickly picked it up and handed it to the elder.

"Thoughtful of you, Redbone." Traveler started hobbling toward the door hanging. Redbone motioned the others to follow Traveler while he gimped along behind with his clubfoot slowing him down.

Eventually, the slow moving parade made it to

the canoe landing. Redbone and Fast Hawk turned the bark canoe over so Traveler could see the inside.

Traveler ran his gnarled hands along the gunwale, bent, and lovingly traced his hand over the painted hand on the bow. The elder slowly stood upright as a tear trickled down his cheek. He stood there on unsteady feet for a few heartbeats before he said, "She is a beauty, my boy. Treat her like a lady, and she will take you far...and she will always protect you." He turned and started up the path toward the palisade on wobbly legs. More tears leaked from his moist brown eyes.

After they were back by the warm fire and Traveler was back on his soft seat, he just sat there with a faraway look on his face. Redbone surmised, correctly, that Traveler was reliving some event from his past.

Corn Stalk ambled into the room using her walking stick to steady her weak knees. Her hair was transitioning from gray to white, and she did not spend the time to keep it under control. Feathery wisps of thin hair stuck out at random from her head.

"Well, have the men solved all the ills of the land?" Corn Stalk inquired rhetorically. Then she looked into Traveler's unfocused eyes. "You are off in your canoe on some unnamed river preparing to trade your trinkets to some unsuspecting maiden for her favors, old man. Am I right?"

"Actually, I was reliving my last ride in MY canoe,

coming into your village just before I handed it to Yellow Hair. I was afraid you would reject me. I guess it worked out for us all in the end, did it not?"

"Do you have any regrets?" she asked.

"None." His answer was one word, but his eyes spoke volumes. She smiled and grasped his hand.

"So, what are your plans, Redbone?" Blue Deer asked. "You are very young to set off down the Spirit River on your own."

"I am not sure. I hear what you are saying, but distant villages are calling me. I do not know what I should do."

"How does your mother feel about you going off trading?" Traveler asked.

"She is totally against it. Father recognizes that my bad foot will never allow me to be a fighting warrior. Mother wants me to learn to be a healer. She says with my strength, I would be good at setting broken bones and dislocations. I have learned some healing plants and can do some first aid, but my heart is in trading. It has been for as long as I can remember."

"Before that, even," Corn Stalk offered to the group. "You should have seen him. The first time he heard Traveler's voice, the boy had only seen three moons. He latched onto that old man and has not let go since. I have never seen the like. But he is a good boy, and even gives his grandmother some love sometimes." She winked and smiled at Redbone.

"You are ready to go on a trading trip right now?" Blue Deer asked.

"I brought several trade goods with me this trip."

"I came to Monongahela Village specifically to see Traveler because the trader who took me in went to the Land of the Ancestors, and I know Traveler would want to know that."

"What happened to him?" inquired Redbone.

"He just got tired, I think. He quit taking his canoe on long trips five sun cycles past and set up a booth on the square in Lenape Town so he could keep trading, although he mostly just talked. One day about three moons past, he did not show up at his booth. I went to see him that morning to say goodbye because I was going to the southern bay. When he was not at his booth, I went to his lodge and found him still in his sleeping skins. I thought he was still sleeping, but when I tried to awaken him, I learned he had gone on. His face wore a smile, so I assume he died in his sleep, peacefully."

"Redbone is sorry to hear you lost your friend and teacher. I am sure you miss him greatly."

"He was like a favorite uncle who teaches you how to fish. Do you understand?"

"Yes. Unfortunately, my uncle left these lands for somewhere across the Great Ocean before I was born. I never had a chance to know him. I have heard great things about him ever since I can remember. I feel deprived of a great teacher. But I have been assured there is no way possible for me to get to where he went with my aunt."

"As you heard earlier, I had the privilege of knowing them both for about a sun cycle. They are great people. Smart, courageous, wise, compassionate—you name every good trait you can think of, and they both possessed it. Too bad they had to leave. I am sure you would have felt the same. I hope they are doing well wherever they are."

"That is what my mother says. My mother and her are twins, you know. Father says they were hard to tell apart, so I know she is beautiful."

"True. I met your mother as well. I had seen ten-and-six summers at that time, so you can believe I was smitten with both of them, even though I only knew your mother for less than a moon, and she was pregnant with you at the time. Still, she was every boy's dream. I probably should not tell you these things."

"Why not? You speak with a straight tongue, there is no need to hide the truth."

"You are very wise for your age. Do you think you would like to come trading in the East with me this summer? Now that I have spent some time with Traveler, I am ready to go back and resume trading back there."

"I came here to spend some time with Traveler. I worry that he will walk the Path to the Ancestors before long." Redbone's manner reminded Blue Deer of how much Redbone idolized Traveler.

"You are still very young. How about you stay here and spend your time with Traveler this summer? Next spring I will come across the trails, and you can come back with me. We will work on your trading and language skills so you will be able go off on your own in the future," Blue Deer suggested.

"I would greatly appreciate that. I really want to spend time with Traveler...and Mother would be happier if Redbone was in Monongahela Village rather than plying the rivers for a few trinkets."

Blue Deer made the sign for a *good trade*.

They both nodded.

"I approve," said Corn Stalk, who had listened to the entire exchange. In the meantime, Traveler was sitting with his back straight and his hands on his knees, but his head was on his chest, and he was sound asleep. She gave him a worried look.

CHAPTER 5
MONONGAHELA VILLAGE

With the Summer Solstice Celebration to take place in Monongahela Village this sun cycle, the whole village was scurrying around making preparations for the big event. Many of the smaller villages making up the Monongahela People were too small and just did not have the resources to host a major event. Therefore, Monongahela Village hosted the majority of the annual summer gatherings.

While Corn Stalk had stepped down as Head Matron of the Monongahela People, she still felt obligated to be involved and worked tirelessly helping her daughter, Corn Silk, the new Head Matron. Corn Silk had learned well from her mother and was regarded as a strong head matron, well-liked by most of her constituents. Still, she accepted Corn Stalk's assistance in preparing for the big celebration.

With still a half-moon to go before the festivities to begin, Corn Stalk spent a day organizing several older children into placing heaping piles of firewood at the locations where the different villages would make their camps around the large meadow where various activities, such as stickball and other games, dances, and feasts would take place. It was an exhausting day for the aging woman.

The joint stiffening disease had slowed Traveler down so much that he was better off sitting by a fire, giving advice, than actually lending a hand in the labor.

The next morning, Corn Stalk awoke complaining of a severe headache. Corn Silk made sure her mother received strong willow bark tea and told her to rest until she felt better.

"Mother, you have done more than your share. Take a day to rest and enjoy sitting with your husband and telling stories," said Corn Silk.

"Thank you, daughter. You are a wise leader. I will take you up on that order," Corn Stalk replied with a weak smile, obviously still in great pain.

During a break in the morning labor, Redbone joined the elders at the fire and sat close behind Traveler. Corn Stalk was telling a story about Traveler bringing Yellow Hair into the village for the first time.

"We women were rushing up to the village wall opening from the planting fields. Sprout, now Strong Elk, came running to me in the field to announce the arrival of a party from Black Bear Village. We were very curious about such a thing happening less than a moon before the Solstice Celebration.

"We were just getting to the village entrance when I see…"

A strange, blank look spread across Corn Stalk's face. Her eyes darted one way, then another, not focusing on anything, alternately rolling back in her head, then around the room.

"Loo…waa…nuk…goot…da," Corn Stalk mumbled incoherently, then toppled into Traveler's lap. Her body shaking while he cradled her, calling her name. As he held her trembling body, she went limp.

"Get Star Keeper here quickly!" Traveler shouted to everyone in the circle of elders. Redbone was the youngest person there. He jumped up and hobbled across the plaza as rapidly as his bad foot would allow toward the healer's lodge.

By the time Redbone returned with Star Keeper, Corn Stalk was laid out on a blanket by the firepit. She lay unmoving but for an occasional twitch of a muscle. Her breathing was shallow and heartbeat barely detectable. Traveler sat by her side, holding her hand and whispering words no one could hear. Corn Stalk had vomited in his lap, but he paid no mind.

The healer had no answers and few ideas. Finally, he spoke. "Her life soul has fled her body and is loose. We need to sing a welcoming song to invite her back before she gets lost."

He began a chant, and the others joined, raising their voices. Soon, everyone in the village had caught onto what was happening to the beloved Corn Stalk, adding their voices. After several choruses of the song, the people began to quiet. Corn Stalk lay motionless and completely relaxed. Her face drooped unnaturally, left side more than the right.

Star Keeper was busy running his fingers over her face and head. He felt nothing unusual and looked at the woman with a perplexed look on his face. The morning slid away with no change. The healer tried different chants, wafted sacred cedar smoke across her body. He squashed differed healing plants between his thumb and finger, then held them to her nose. Nothing changed.

By midafternoon, with no change, Star Keeper declared she should be moved to her own bed. The familiar surroundings may call her soul back to her body.

As the sun was setting, Corn Stalk quietly died. Traveler wept. All of Monongahela Village wept. All of Corn Stalk's numerous family members hacked their hair off unevenly with knives in mourning. Wails of sorrow emanated from the Corn Clan long-house and across the village until the next dawn. Corn Stalk's name would not be spoken again. She would be referred to as the *Beloved Former Head Matron.*

War Chief Red Oak, Strong Elk, and four other warriors carried Corn Stalk's body on a litter to the village charnel house where Star Keeper would prepare her body for burial. Corn Silk declared that Corn Stalk's funeral would take place on the first day of the Solstice Celebration so that all the Monongahela People could mourn their former Head Matron. She would be buried along the north wall of the Corn Clan longhouse, close to where three of her predecessors were buried. Runners were sent to each village to inform them of Corn Stalk's mysterious passing. Fast Hawk volunteered and took a one-man canoe up the Ohi-yo River to New Long Pine and Black Bear Villages.

Rather than taking the role of runner and going back to New Long Pine Village, Redbone elected to stay with Traveler. The elder was grateful for the young man's company, although their conversations were few and subdued when they spoke. Just having the young man in his presence helped Traveler cope with the gaping hole in his heart. Traveler had hacked his thinning white hair and now looked as if he had donned a wispy cloud for a hat.

In the following days, Traveler treated Redbone like a cherished nephew. The elder talked about the finer points of being a trader. Things like how to organize his packs to balance a canoe and move a heavily laden canoe through all kinds of water by oneself. He taught the young man the keys to learning how to communicate in trader pigeon in many different tongues. He talked about where the friendliest people could be found and what goods were favored in what parts of Turtle Island. He talked about the great civilizations on some of the rivers, the treacherous Grandmother River, majesty of the high Shining Mountains, the diversity of peoples in the Tenasee River lands, the impressive flow of the Grandfather River, the beaches and people of the Southern Ocean, and the old knowledge of the people along the Great Eastern Ocean. Finally, he admitted his regrets that he never traveled among the stone temple builders west of the Caddo lands, or to the ice covered lands of the far north where great white bears live.

Redbone hung on every word and committed the stories to his remarkable memory. He knew Traveler's time was limited. He was grateful for the time the elder was willing to spend with him. Traveler was even inspired to walk all the way to the landing to inspect Redbone's bark canoe several times.

"A well-crafted vessel. This canoe will last you many sun cycles if you care for it properly," said Traveler. He then instructed Redbone how to boil pine or birch sap to paint the seams and skin of the boat. Redbone did not mention that Red Hand had already showed him how to do that.

FIVE DAYS before the opening ceremonies of the Solstice Celebration, Red Hand, Bright Star, Bright Moon, and Fast Hawk arrived at Monongahela

Village. The rest of those coming from New Long Pine Village would be along in a couple days.

Bright Star wanted to spend some private time with Corn Silk before the crowds arrived. Already many had beaten her to the biggest village among the Monongahela People. Still, she was able to get the details on the Beloved Former Head Matron's mysterious death.

Redbone was curious why his mother did not question why he stayed in Monongahela Village rather than going home where he could at least get his ceremonial clothes for the funeral. He knew that he should have been the runner to inform his mother of the tragedy.

When he got her alone, Redbone asked, "Mother, were you not upset that Fast Hawk came to give you the news of the Beloved Former Head Matron's passing? Or that I chose to stay here instead of hurrying home?"

"Son, after my childhood and the things in my past, I am the last person to ask why another person chooses the path they take. I completely understand why you wanted to stay with Traveler. You are tied to him like my sister was tied to Wolf. I have no desire to question why power works the way it does. I am confident all things are planned by forces we do not need to understand. And please forgive me for trying to redirect your path in the past. I should have known better.

"Now, your father, he will try to shame you for

neglecting your own family. I told him that you must follow your own trail."

"Thank you, Mother. I will try to make Father understand. You should know that next summer, I will be going with Blue Deer into the Lenape lands to trade. I will probably be gone a full sun cycle."

"Is that the Blue Deer who traveled with Long Cat?"

"Yes. He will come here to get me so we can travel together. He said when I have learned to trade with his people up and down the coast, he will bring me back. Hopefully, I will have enough coastal goods to go west."

"I see. Well, be easy on your father. He is also very worried about Bright Moon, who wishes to be a great warrior like her aunt who no longer lives among us. It seems his children are walking different paths than he had planned for them."

"My path has been clear as long as I can remember," Redbone said.

"Even longer, son." Bright Star thought back to the first time Redbone heard Traveler's voice.

"I will be truthful when Father questions me."

"That is all anyone can ask. Now let us go enjoy some roast turkey." Bright Star was happy to have that conversation behind her. *Yes, I will miss him when he goes to follow his calling, but how can I stop him? Corn Stalk did all she could to stop me and my sister from becoming warriors, but we did as we were destined. If spirits have planned for Redbone to become a river trader, who am I to try to stop him? Worse things could become of a man. Think of Traveler. Sister said that he was always an honorable man. He was old enough to be my grandfather when he finally settled down, but he honored and cared for Corn Stalk until her end. I hope the rest of his days are peaceful.*

Before the sun set, Red Hand finally got Redbone alone and away from curious ears. "Why have you stayed away for all this time? I am disappointed by your lack of responsibility. There are many things you can and should be doing around your home village. Then, when the Head Matron died, you let Fast Hawk deliver the message while you stayed here, doing nothing but hanging around bothering Traveler. What have you to say for yourself?"

"Father, I know you are upset that Bright Moon is set on becoming a fierce warrior. It seems to me that some force outside of our human knowledge is driving her. If that is the case, how can you stop her? Is it so hard to believe that we each have a destiny? Your own destiny was to not blindly follow an evil war chief. Instead, you followed instincts that led you to Mother. Then, at great risk to yourself, you helped Mother and her sister fulfill a destiny that was even more treacherous. But now, you find it difficult to let your children follow their destiny. I have felt the call to become a river trader as long as I can remember. You know that. And you know there is no better teacher than Traveler. Now, I feel Traveler will be walking the Path of the Ancestors before long. He seems to enjoy sharing his knowledge with me. How can this be wrong?"

"You knew I would be trying to shame you and concocted that response. All this talk about spirits and other unknown forces shaping our destinies is folly. The only person controlling us is us. We do, of our own free will, what we do. Blaming it on *unknown forces* is simply a means to justify our actions. Fine, if you want to become a river trader when you get older and mature, so be it. But right now, you still have family and clan responsibilities that are your duties. You need to understand that, too. And so does your sister." Red Hand was feeling his anger taking control and tried to cool off before he said something he might regret.

"I cannot believe you, of all people, would say these things, Father!" Redbone could feel himself losing control as well.

Bright Star saw her husband and son arguing and went to investigate since she could not hear their words.

"What is the trouble, my men?" asked Bright Star.

"None of your concern, woman!" Red Hand tersely replied.

"Oh, I think if my husband is berating my son, it is most certainly my concern. Either my son has done something egregious, such as stealing something valuable, or my husband is making a mountain out of a molehill, like blaming my son for learning how to live his future."

"He has been shirking his duties at home while lazing around Monongahela Village for two moons," said Red Hand.

"So, it is my husband making a mountain out of a molehill. Bright Star recalls a time when Red Hand slipped away from his duties in Black Bear Village to spend time with a maiden from an enemy camp. In his case, and in the case of my son, they were preparing themselves for a better future. Perhaps it is time for Red Hand to understand that Redbone does not follow the same trail as the other young warriors. If the best elder for guiding his future is in Mononga-hela Village, then that is where he needs to be.

"There are many young warriors in New Long Pine Village who can do the things Redbone needs to do there. But there is only one trader who can impart the wisdom Redbone needs to prepare him for a life on the rivers. And that trader will not walk among men much longer. If Redbone can learn from him before he walks the Path of the Ancestors, then here is where Redbone needs to be. Does this make sense, husband?" She took the war chief's hand and held it tenderly while she looked into his smoldering eyes.

Red Hand's countenance softened. He looked into his son's eyes and saw a determination so familiar from long past that his knees felt weak. He smiled at his son and said, "A river trader?"

"Yes, Father," Redbone replied with confidence.

"Now I understand." Red Hand looked into Bright Star's eyes. "Now that a wise Head Matron has pointed to the error of my assumptions, I retract what I said about your duties and ask how I can help you follow your trail?"

"You have already given me a valuable canoe. And all the things you have taught me over the years have given me the foundation to being a good man. I am in your debt now."

"I have only done what a father should do for his son. And your debt is paid when you teach your own son how to be a good man. Those things apply whether your son is to be a great war leader, a civil chief, or a river trader. Good men are needed to fill all moccasins."

"With that settled, can we head over to the main plaza? There are many who wish to catch up with our happenings, just as we need to hear their news." The couple started for the big field where the evening fire was just being lit. Redbone limped along beside them, not letting his bad foot slow him down.

CHAPTER 6
A FUNERAL

Star Keeper, dressed in a bright red cape flowing from his neck to the ground, stood before the crowd of hundreds of mourners with his arms outstretched and raised to the sky. His first duty on this day was to officially open the Summer Solstice Celebration at Monongahela Village.

His red cape was decorated with shell spirals, chevrons, crossed bars, and symbols of every clan from the ten-and-eight villages that made up the Monongahela nation. His face was painted half red and half white. A shell gorget hung on a braided human hair necklace. The palm-sized white clam shell displayed a sunburst carved and painted yellow. His long dark-brown hair was twisted into a tight bun at the back of his head. A red line followed the part from his forehead and over the top of his head. Four eagle feathers hung from the bun at the back of his head. Each feather was painted in one of the four sacred colors.

As the sun broke over the hills east of the village, he lowered his arms and voiced, "People of the Monongahela nation, we gather here this day to begin the celebration of the longest day of the current sun cycle. It is the time we express our thanks to Brother Sun for bringing us the light and warmth to raise the three sisters, to grow the fruit, nuts, and plants that nourish our bodies and heal our infirmities.

"We will begin this Solstice Celebration by honoring the beloved Head Matron who so recently passed from this world. Today we will honor her life and sing the songs to help her find her way to the Path of the Ancestors. New Head Matron, Corn Silk, daughter of the deceased, will begin the tribute."

The Shaman and Healer of Monongahela Village, Star Keeper, stepped aside as the new head matron walked to the speaker's place in front of the crowd.

"Today, we gather to raise our voices in tribute to the woman who served our people as Head Matron of the Corn Clan before she was chosen as Head Matron of all our people. This great woman was more than a head matron to me. She was my mother. She healed my injuries and dried my tears as a child. She loved me and my siblings as only a mother could. And, yes, she meted out discipline to us when we deserved it. She was everything a mother should be.

"Then she stepped up to the position of Head

Matron of Monongahela Village and the whole nation. She became the mother of all of us and performed her duties for more sun cycles than any head matron the Monongahela People have ever known. She led our people in times of war and times of peace, and in times of scarcity and times of plenty. She was always a solid force of reason through it all.

"Today, I stand in front of the largest crowd ever gathered for the Summer Solstice Celebration. My mother made that happen. The Monongahela nation is larger than it has ever been. This was made possible by her strong leadership and care for each of us under her protection. I pray to the Creator that I am able continue in her footsteps. I promise to do my very best to fill her moccasins."

As Corn Silk ended her speech, a flute began a sorrowful tune. The crowd began a death song:

Oh, Spirit of My Life,
Lead Me Up, Up, Up!
Light The Path Before Me,
That I May Follow
Across the Bridge,
To the Land Of Those Who
Have Gone Before Me.
Oh, Spirits Who I Have Known,
Show Me The Way,
So That I Will Not
Fall Into The Darkness.
Oh, Spirits Of My Life,

> *Lead Me Up, Up, Up,*
> *Into Your Light.*
> *Guide Me On The Trail*
> *To The Ancestors!*
> *Lead Me Up, Up, Up,*
> *To The Campfires*
> *Of The Dead!*
> *Lead Me Up, Up, Up!*

When the song ended, Star Keeper stepped forward and said, "War Chief Red Oak, I believe you have some words to share?"

Red Oak walked up to Star Keeper's side. He was dressed in a midthigh length buckskin war shirt dyed red with fringes down both arms and along the bottom hem. Shell bead chevrons decorated the shoulders. Similar beaded depictions of corn ears lined up along and just above the bottom hem. Light, tan-colored buckskin fringed leggings covered his legs. They were decorated with shell spirals and chevrons featuring beads of the four sacred colors. He wore a buckskin breechclout dyed white with a short red fringe. His chopped black hair fell unevenly around his head. His forehead was painted black, a red band painted across the middle of his face including his ears, and from the bottom of his nose to his neck was bright white.

"Friends of all the Monongahela villages and all the visitors from other lands, we thank you for coming to pay tribute to my beloved grandmother's life. We all know she was a special person and leader. Each of us pray for guidance that we may live up to her honorable standards.

"In her honor, the Clans of Monongahela Village have prepared a feast to share with all of you. Along the south side of this field, you will see a series of awnings. Food and drink will be served to all of you. But please be patient, as there are many guests and not all can be served at once. While you are enjoying the food, a party of us will proceed to into the Village to tend to the burial of our beloved former Head Matron.

"When the burial is completed and the feast is over, the children's games and contests will take place on this field. Tomorrow, the adult stickball games will start right here on this field. Other ceremonies will be conducted over the next three days and nights. And, of course, each night there will be dancing starting with the sunset.

"With that, I release you to go fill your plates."

The masses drifted toward the booths where the food and drink were being served while members of the deceased's family and certain clan officials followed Corn Silk through the palisade opening to the north side of the Corn Clan longhouse.

They gathered around an oval-shaped hole that had been dug just north of the north wall of the oval-shaped longhouse at approximately the center. The hole was about ten hands deep and eight hands by six hands with the shorter side parallel to the longhouse. The dirt removed to dig the hole was in several baskets lined up along the outside of the longhouse wall. The bottom of the hole was leveled, and a red woven-grass mat was placed in it.

When all the officials and guests had arrived, Star Keeper formally introduced each person, giving their name, clan lineage, and relationship to the deceased Head Matron. All of the female members of the immediate family were first, followed by her husband, Traveler, who had been adopted into the Corn Clan since he previously declared no clan, nor could he even name what people he had been born into.

The introductions took two hands of time. Too long of time for Traveler to stand. A special log seat covered with a mountain lion hide had been provided for him. Other elderly members were provided logs seat with deer hide covers.

After the introductions and placement of the seated guests, two older boys dressed in white-colored deer hide capes carried an oval-shaped bundle around the longhouse from the direction of the charnel house where Star Keeper had prepared the body for burial.

The bones had been cleaned of all soft tissue and were arranged into a flat, oval shape with the skull situated in the middle, on top. A red ochre spiral and an ear of corn adorned the top and temples of the cleaned skull. The bundle was then wrapped in a bag made from several red-dyed fawn skins sewn together. Her shell gorget with an etched ear of corn on it was place at the point of her lower jaw before the bundle was wrapped. The young men placed the bundle close to the side of the hole, where it would remain until all the speakers had their say.

Corn Silk led off the graveside eulogies, followed by Traveler, whose tears were steadily flowing

\down his wrinkled cheeks. After Traveler, each of the former Head Matron's children had their say. Traveler paid no attention as former husbands, all deceased, were mentioned. When the family members finished their speeches, a long line of close associates made their way to pay verbal tribute to the deceased.

When all the speeches were finished, Star Keeper climbed down into the hole. The two boys carefully lowered the bundled bones down to Star Keeper who arranged the bundle so that it was oriented with the eye sockets pointed toward the east. When the bundle was placed just right, Star Keeper said a prayer and climbed back out of the grave. The log was removed. Star Keeper spoke two more ritual prayers, then dismissed the guests. Three boys then filled the grave until it was just a slightly raised mound of disturbed dirt. The deceased Head Matron now rested among other female members of her lineage who had walked the Path of the Ancestors before her.

CHAPTER 7
SUMMER SOLSTICE

"I can only guess how deep your sorrow is, Traveler," Redbone told his aging idol.

"My sorrow is not for me, Redbone. I weep for all those who will never sit in her company. All those grandchildren and great grandchildren who will never know what an amazing person she was, what a great leader she was. She touched so many lives for a long time. But there will be generations that will never have the privilege of her in their lives. Does that make sense to a young person like you?"

"Yes, of course. I did know her, some, and I loved her more than I can express. I know mother said she was one of the finest people she ever knew. Mother said all the nagging the Head Matron did to her and her sister was out of love, not trying to use her power."

"Hah, no power anyone ever wielded would

change your aunt's mind." Traveler's eyes misted as he looked into the past.

Redbone noted Traveler's voice had weakened in the days since his wife had passed. *How much longer will he be with us?*

"Do you think they made it to Yellow Hair's people? Mother says she just knows, somehow, that they are alive and well. She says that Aunt Bright Moon has children, too. But she cannot tell me how she knows that."

"They are twins. Sometimes twins have some extra sense so they can feel things their twin feels, no matter how far apart they are. But I would not be surprised at anything your mother and aunt say. They both have ways that I cannot explain...and I have seen many things in my life."

Now Redbone noticed that Traveler's voice became a little stronger as he talked about his mother and aunt. "Do you think they will ever come back?"

"I have no idea. Only the spirits guiding them could answer that question. He said he wanted to open trade relations between our people and his, but unless he found enough men who would trade and not fight, he would not bring them here. My guess is, he has not found those men yet."

"That is a shame. I think I would want to trade with him."

"He described some fantastic things I would like

to see. Those big animals they ride on must be a sight, for sure."

"They ride animals? Like deer?"

"Bigger," he said. "More like moose, but with no antlers."

"Amazing! Now I really want to go there."

"Yellow Hair tried to explain their great canoes to me, but I just could not picture them. Even after he drew pictures for me. Just too different than anything I have seen. On the other hand, he was astonished when we arrived in Cahokia. He had never seen anything like that either. He said their animals would drag those big logs, so men did not need to carry them. I would like to see that, too!"

To Redbone, Traveler seemed to be getting younger as he talked about Yellow Hair. *I wonder if I should keep him going.*

Suddenly Traveler started coughing. He could not stop and began wheezing between coughs. Redbone quickly went to Traveler's side and patted his back— something his mother had taught him.

After several heartbeats, the elder's coughing slowed, and he began to catch his breath, though he was still wheezing and had a hard time getting a lungful of air. When Traveler finally stopped coughing, he looked at Redbone through bloodshot, watery eyes, and said, "I think it is time for this old man to stop talking and rest a bit. Come back tomorrow, and we will talk some more."

Redbone agreed and left the longhouse. In the

plaza, he saw his mother discussing something with Corn Silk. He hated to interrupt but limped over by his mother.

"You look worried. What is it, son?" Bright Moon asked.

"I did not want to interrupt you, Mother. Maybe it can wait."

"It looks important. We were just talking about how your sister put all the young men to shame in the games three days past. What is on your mind?" Now Bright Star was starting to worry.

"It...it is Traveler. We were talking, and he started coughing. It was terrible. He could not breathe, and when he did, he was wheezing something awful. I patted and rubbed his back like you taught me. Finally, he stopped wheezing and told me he needed to rest. But I worry about him. He is nothing but skin and bone. He just seems so old. But when we were talking about you, Aunt Bright Moon, and Yellow Hair, he seemed to get stronger, even younger. Then he started coughing. I thought he was going to die." A tear rolled down his cheek.

"He is very old, but he seems much older after losing his wife. Is he all right now?" she asked.

"A little, I think. He said he needed to rest, so I left him lying on his bed platform," Redbone replied.

"We all worry about him. It was bad enough to lose Mother. I would hate to see him go so soon after her. I better go check on him. Thank you for spending time with him, Redbone. I know he enjoys your company," said Corn Silk. She walked through the door hanging into the darkness of the longhouse.

"Let us go back to our camp. We are preparing to head back upriver tomorrow. Will you be going with us or staying here?" Bright Star asked.

"I am not sure. I want to make sure Traveler is all right. I need to see what Fast Hawk has planned. He seems to be spending a lot of time with that girl, Green Lark of the Wolf Clan.

"I noticed that. So did his mother. Changes never stop coming, it seems. I cannot help thinking back to the day when you two fought like you were trying to kill each other. He broke that odd bone on your foot, and when you punched him, he bit off a piece of his tongue. He still talks with a lisp. At the time, I thought you two would be bitter enemies for life. But within two moons, you were best friends. I am glad you made up. Now he may be moving to this village."

"We were just boys and had much to learn. We have grown close, and I only wish him happiness and success in all he does. He is strong and will be a great warrior for the Wolf Clan. Whether it is in New Long Pine or Monongahela Village is yet to be determined, but I think she sees him as he sees her. At the dances, they clung to each other."

"Will you miss next Solstice Celebration at River Birch Village?" she carefully asked.

"I expect to. Blue Deer will come for me in the Awakening Moon after the snowmelt floods have quieted in the rivers. I will be gone a whole sun cycle, I expect."

"Your mother will miss you. So will your sister and father. But I think he understands now and will support you any way he can."

"Thank you, Mother, for helping me show him what it means to me to become a trader like Grandfather Traveler."

"I admire you for following your dreams, son. You are making your mother proud."

"Many think I am a fool and will come back like a starving dog begging for scraps. I wish to prove them wrong."

"You will. A mother can feel the strength in her children."

"I am no longer a child."

"You will always be a child in your mother's heart, my son. That is how the creator made mothers. Like the earth, we create life and cherish what we create until we no longer draw breath." Bright Star put a strong arm around Redbone's back and pulled him to her.

He laid his arm over her shoulder and hugged her back. "And I will always cherish you, Mother.

"In the Lenape lands, I hope to find people who remember Bright Moon and Yellow Hand. Red Oak tells me they made many friends among them when he escorted them up the Lenape River. Their yellow-haired son, Acorn, was an instant attraction everywhere they went after the boy was born."

Tears flowed from Bright Star's eyes as she thought about her sister. *I wish I could have known that boy. He is Redbone's age. He will probably be big and strong, like his father. I hope Yellow Hair's god is watching over all of them. I think my sister has several children by now. That is what Wolf told her. I find it odd that Wolf came to her, but never to me. Perhaps she needed more protection than I did, or maybe she was the chosen one.*

"Are you well, Mother? I was asking you about leaving this village, but it was like your souls left your body. Your look was strange, and tears wet your cheeks." His voice reflected worry.

"Just thinking about my sister and how much I miss her. Nothing for you to fret about." She tried to sound confident. "Let us go see what mischief your sister has gotten into. And then we need to get back here. Our family is invited to Corn Silk's longhouse for our last evening meal in Monongahela Village."

"My sister? Mischief? Surely nothing more than breaking the Head Matron's son's arm or leg!"

"Do not even think it! We better hurry."

When they got to their camp they found Bright Moon excitedly telling Red Hand how she killed a mountain lion that was stalking the same deer she was. She was talking rapidly while skinning the big cat that she had dragged into camp on a litter she made for the purpose.

"Never a dull moment with that one!" Bright Star told Redbone as they approached.

"Another successful hunt," Bright Star announced her and Redbone's arrival.

"This cat thought he was going to steal my deer. I got him and the deer ran off unharmed. Now I can make a cat claw necklace!" Bright Moon exclaimed.

"Be sure to put a claw and a tooth in your spirit bundle. That cat's spirit will appreciate the honor," said Redbone.

"Good idea, brother! Thank you." Bright Moon smiled from ear to ear. A streak of blood was smeared across her face from her swiping a bloody hand over her mouth.

Red Hand looked on with a wry grin shaking his head at the antics of his almost grown children. He took Bright Star into his arms as she walked up.

"We have raised sedate, orderly clan leaders, my wife. Our son will own the river trade in places we have never heard of, and our daughter will outhunt, outrun, and outfight any warrior in the entire nation." Red Hand squeezed his wife closer.

"Something to be proud of," she snickered.

At evening meal in the Corn Clan longhouse, Bright Star and her family were sitting in honored guest places along the central firepit. Every person in attendance had chopped their hair unevenly in mourning. Plates with elk steaks, boiled cattail and arrowhead roots, and corn cakes had been served along with sassafras and mint tea. When the plates had been cleared by Corn Silk's servants, the Head Matron looked at Bright Moon and asked, "I understand you had quite an adventure today. Care to relate your story?"

"It was nothing, Head Matron. I was following a deer, and a mountain lion intruded. I was able to take him down with one arrow. It was hard work dragging him back to camp, but he was not as heavy as the deer I was stalking," Bright Moon answered.

"Hardly *nothing*. You are what, ten-and-one sun cycles? What on earth are you doing out hunting by yourself in a strange forest? You are just a child."

Bright Moon was wearing her fine-tanned doeskin dress with Water Plant Clan symbols embroidered in shell beads on the front. Her hair flowed unevenly down over her ears and neck.

"Head Matron, I have seen ten-and-two summers and have been hunting alone for at least a sun cycle. I have worked hard to become the hunter my aunt with the same name was before she went with her husband to a foreign land."

"And what of your clan responsibilities? Have you shunned them like your aunt did?"

"All I can say is, some of us are born to be clan matrons and some of us are born to follow a different trail."

"You are still a child, what do you know of trails? Obviously someone has neglected to impress upon you the importance of your clan and family in the future of New Long Pine Village and the Mononga-hela People."

"I would answer that by saying that the future

of New Long Pine Village and the Monongahela People will depend on a strong warrior society. I understand the northern Haudenosaunee are becoming more numerous and aggressive. We will need to counter with stronger defenses than we have now. My intention is to be a part of those strong defenses. Aunt Water Mint has provided daughters who will be strong in clan and village leadership. But my cousins will depend on a strong war chief with strong deputies. That is where I fit in."

Corn Silk gaped open-mouthed at the insolent child sitting at her firepit talking like a seasoned war chief. Bright Star looked at her daughter with pride in her eyes. Red Hand looked like he wanted to slink out of the longhouse. Redbone looked at his lap with a big smile on his face.

"Very well, walk your own trail. Apparently your mother approves. Your life will probably be a short one, and I pray none of those Haudenosaunee warriors capture you while you are out wandering around hunting dangerous animals. I understand they are not kind to their enemy captives, especially women. I am done talking about this subject." Corn Silk made it clear the conversation was over.

On the way back to their camp, Bright Star said to her daughter, "Well, you surely did not back down from the Head Matron."

Before Bright Moon could answer, Red Hand said, "I cannot believe you talked to the Head Matron like you did. She could make you a slave with that attitude. What were you thinking?"

"I answered with truth. Something you have always stressed. Like my aunt, I was not born a sedate clan matron. I was born to walk a trail filled with excitement and danger. I will not sit humbly while some powerful person berates me for being who I am. I have no problem avoiding contact with that woman in the future. She will only appreciate me when I put an arrow into the enemy warrior rushing toward her with a raised warclub in his hand. Afterward, she will want me gone because I am not gentle enough for her company."

"Somewhere there must be a happy place where you can be tough and still show respect to powerful people," Red Hand offered.

"That can be a fine line, my husband. Moon is right that the Head Matron will never appreciate what she wants to be. Just as the former Head Matron insisted that my sister and I were crazy for attempting what we had planned—right up to the day we returned following a successful war walk. And you were a big part of that. Never forget that people are not made from a clay mold. Each of us must do what it says in here." She pointed to her chest, a movement barely visible in the weak moonlight obscured by a veil of thin clouds.

"Let us concentrate on getting some sleep so we can get an early start for home tomorrow," said Bright Star.

"As you probably suspect, I will be staying here, Mother. I think Traveler will be walking with the Ancestors before the coming winter ends. I feel obligated to stay with him a while longer," Redbone said.

"Yes, we all thought you would. Learn what you can from him before it is too late, but do not pester him. Take the information he shares freely, but do not beg him if he is too tired, or unwilling, to share something with you," Red Hand admonished his son.

"I would never push him, Father. He says talking to me about his past awakens his memory and makes him feel younger. I think he enjoys having a student." Redbone seemed to walk taller with less of a limp when talking about Traveler.

The sky was showing the first hints of a new day when Redbone and Bright Moon began loading their family possessions into their big dugout. They distributed the weight so the boat would float level in the water with Red Hand in the rear and Bright Star in the middle, even though she was still stronger than Bright Moon. The girl insisted on the front position where she would need to work harder than the middle position, and so that she would be forced to learn more about guiding the canoe upriver.

After loading what they could, they went back to the camp and began heating corn gruel and leftover venison stew for morning meal. Before the elk stomach bags with the gruel and stew were warm, Red Hand and Bright Star crawled out of the tent.

Bright Star had a deer hide blanket wrapped

around her, and her cropped black hair stuck out in all directions. High moccasins covered her feet and shins. Red Hand had a long sleeve tanned buckskin shirt that hung down to midthigh. He wore a breech-clout but no leggings. Ankle high moccasins covered his feet. His hair was also chopped and hung unevenly around his head. Neither wore any decoration that indicated their rank of Head Matron and War Chief of New Long Pine Village.

"We should be on the river before the sun appears over the hills this morning," Red Hand casually said.

"Is the tea warm yet?" Bright Star asked Bright Moon.

"Soon, Mother. You look as if you did not sleep well," replied Bright Moon.

"Anxious to get home, I guess."

"A long day on the river should fix that," Redbone offered.

The sky was now a pale blue as the day began. Tendrils of woodsmoke rising above the palisade told them the village was waking up. Already a few men were filing out of the village to begin a day hunting, fishing, or cutting shafts for arrows, lances, and other tools for precuring food.

Women would soon follow on their way to the fields to tend to the three sisters. Although the corn had been planted first, then the beans that would climb the corn stalks for support, and the squash planted in the spaces between the hills of corn to save water and control unwanted plants, pesky weeds would invade that needed to be hoed away from the desired plants so they would grow healthy.

Soon enough, the family had eaten and finished packing for the five-day trip up the Ohi-yo River to New Long Pine Village. Just as they were finishing, Corn Silk, her husband, former War Chief Wolf Tracker, new War Chief Red Oak, his wife, Primrose, and Strong Elk came out of the village to bid them farewell.

Bright Moon kept her eyes averted, worried about being chastised by Corn Silk, but the meeting was cordial without any negative words. The Head Matron wished them safe travels, abundant harvests, and peace until their next meeting. She even hugged Bright Moon and wished her well. The girl wished the Head Matron a prosperous summer.

Finally, they shoved off and were paddling vigorously to push the canoe across the Spirit River and into the channel of the Ohi-yo. Those left on the bank waved their goodbyes before going back into the village. Redbone and Strong Elk brought up the rear and talked about hunting for the Corn Clan.

In the Corn Clan longhouse, Redbone found Traveler sitting on his special log seat with the mountain lion skin covering.

"Are you well this morning, Elder?" Redbone asked Traveler.

"Fit enough to sit up and drink sweetened tea. I thought you would be on the river headed north this morning," the elder replied in his scratchy *old man* voice.

"I wanted to make sure you are feeling well before I leave. Besides, I promised Strong Elk I would help him hunt to replace some of the meat we have been eating around here for the past several days." Redbone smiled when he saw the corners of Traveler's mouth turn upward.

"I will leave you the steaks if you bring me some fresh liver. The steaks do not chew so well in my old mouth these days," Traveler declared.

"Count on it. Is there anything I can get or do for you before I go, Elder?"

"No. I appreciate your concern and be sure to come back. Your enthusiasm for starting your life as a trader makes me feel younger. And before you part for the Lenape lands, I have some things to tell you."

"I will return with fresh liver and eager ears, Elder." With that, Redbone turned and left Traveler alone. The rest of the longhouse was busy with the morning's work.

CHAPTER 8

TRADES

Strong Elk and Redbone made their way to the central firepit, each on the end of a pole with a fat deer carcass hanging between them. It was an awkward carry because Strong Elk was nearly a hand taller than Redbone and the shorter man had to limp on every step to compensate for his deformed foot.

Redbone left Strong Elk to deal with hanging the deer so women could skin and prepare the meat for cooking or drying. He leaned his bow against a post and went into the Corn Clan longhouse and to Traveler's chamber.

"As promised!" Redbone slid the pack off his shoulder, set it on the floor, and pulled the deer's stomach from the pack, and took the cleaned, still warm, liver out of the stomach.

Traveler smiled and slid off the sleeping platform. "Looks like we should go to the firepit and share this treat." He indicated to Redbone to wrap the fresh liver back into the stomach and bring it out to where the crowd was gathering around the hanging deer carcass.

Once at the firepit, Redbone held the liver out to Traveler, who took his knife from his belt sheath and sliced a chunk off. The elder held the chunk up to his mouth and gnawed on it with his toothless gums until he had a bite sized sliver in his mouth. "Good!" he garbled with blood and saliva running from the corners of his mouth and down over his chin.

The rest of the liver did not last long as Redbone passed it to the people standing around watching the few women skinning the deer.

When Traveler finished his piece of liver, he said something only Red Oak could hear as the elder leaned over to talk in his ear.

"I need you attention people!" Red Oak announced to the crowd. "Traveler has announced there will be a trading session in the plaza tomorrow featuring goods that Redbone here gathered around New Long Pine Village and up the Ohi-yo River. Come out tomorrow midmorning to see what this new trader has to offer. I think you will be pleasantly surprised."

Someone called out, "If Traveler trusts him, so does Tall Hawk!" Nods of approval ran through the group.

Redbone stood flabbergasted. He was worried about trading anything right after the solstice, with all the trading that took place during the celebration. *Now, the spotlight will be on me, and I will need to perform! How could Traveler do this?* He looked over at Traveler to see him looking back with a wide toothless smile on his face.

Then people started to walk up to Redbone. "What kinds of goods do you have, boy?" was the typical question.

His standard answer was, "I have some deer and elk skins, a few beaver, foxes, coyote, and a wolverine."

Someone would ask, "Do you have any mink?"

"Yes."

"Any otter?"

"Yes."

"Any weapons?"

"I have some arrows, lance shafts, and chert nodules."

And so it went for a time, until Red Oak raised his voice, "All right, we get the idea. Redbone has many things you want. Come out tomorrow, check the quality, and make your trades. Traveler and I will be here to make sure no one tries to take advantage of Redbone because he is young and new to the trade."

"Thank you, War Chief. My throat was getting dry, answering all the questions," said Redbone.

From the crowd, Redbone noticed Fast Hawk and Green Lark moving his way.

"Sounds like tomorrow will be a busy day!" Fast Hawk called when he got close to Redbone.

"Yes, I hope the people are not disappointed," replied Redbone.

"They better not be. I helped tan many of those skins, and I know they are high quality!" Fast Hawk said, with a grin.

Fast Hawk turned to Green Lark and said something.

"On behalf of the Hawk Clan and my mother, Head Matron Singing Lark, we would ask Redbone to join us for evening meal in the Hawk Clan longhouse tonight. Can you make it?"

Redbone looked to Traveler, who he knew was listening. Traveler nodded.

"I would be happy to join your clan for tonight's meal."

"Good, and in the morning, I will help you set your things out for the trade," Fast Hawk said.

Redbone found it impossible to get to sleep. Every time he closed his eyes, images of tomorrow's trade session popped into his head. One thought brought great profit and glory, the next brought failure and despair. One minute he thought his goods would be praised and highly sought, the next brought open criticism, and he was run out of the square and told never to return. He tossed and turned all night.

Fast Hawk tried to sleep in the tent with his friend but soon grew impatient with Redbone's anxiety. He moved his blankets out of the tent and laid them in the trampled field more than one hundred paces away. Once out in the quiet, he slept like the dead.

Redbone finally gave up and went for a walk along the river. It was a warm night with a clear sky and a light southern breeze. The stars and half-moon gave Redbone more than enough light to follow a trail along the riverbank after leaving the cleared fields east of Monongahela Village.

After picking his way along the trail for more than a hand of time, Redbone came to a small creek that drained into the river. Just on the other side of the creek, where it flowed into the river, was a large rock with a flat surface. He thought he might sit on the rock and rest. In looking for a place to cross the creek, he found an old trail that followed the creek to the south. Despite debris and a few sprouts along the trail, it was easy to follow in the moonlight. Curiosity led him to walk that trail.

The trail followed the creek for a time, then crossed the creek and led toward a steep hill. When he neared the dark base of the hill, he saw the trail went through a cut in the weathered rocks that had long past split away from the rocky wall. The cleared path turned to his left along the base of the wall between it and the separated section.

After several steps along that trail, something shiny just above the leafy floor of the trail caught his eye. He bent down to see what he had found. It was an old arrow point. The sinew tying it to the shaft was rotted, but a broken shaft lay there. In the dark, it was hard to see, but it appeared that the arrow was not shot from a bow. It was just lying there like it was broken by slamming against the rock that was on the steep side of the trail. Very odd. He put the arrow point and both pieces of the shaft in his pack. The shaft felt fragile, like it was half rotted.

Then he continued along the trail to the east. Soon, he came to a pile of burned logs. *Another oddity!* The moon was directly overhead now, and even with a half-moon, it was very light. He began seeing bits of trash among the burned logs. A piece of rotted, albeit tanned, elk hide. Pieces of a broken pot. Coals from old fires. Pieces of discarded clothing. Some rotted pieces of buckskin, some chewed by mice. *Someone lived here before the fire. I wonder what their story was. It does not look like it was too long past. Maybe someone in the village knows. I feel a strange attachment to this place. Another mystery!*

The burned lodge seemed to be the end of the trail. Suddenly it dawned on him—this is where Mother grew up! The stories she shared with Water Mint and Tallow. This was the hermit lodge they kept while Aunt Bright Moon learned to fight the evil war chief. All he could think about was that burned pile of logs that had once been Mother's home.

He picked up a piece of a broken clay pot and put into his pack along with the arrow he had picked up earlier. He vowed he would come back in the light of day to search for more artifacts of his mother's previous life.

Satisfied he had found all he could in the moonlight, he turned to make his way back to his camp downriver. The trail was even easier to follow on his way back. As he worked his way down the river, the moon slowly moved toward the western horizon. The time passed quickly as his mind was occupied by his discovery. The first person he would tell would be Traveler. Surely he had visited that hidden lodge.

He arrived at his camp before the first hints of a new day made an appearance in the starlit sky. Expecting to lay awake thinking of the new day, he fell asleep before he pulled his blanket over his shoulders.

"You are wasting the best part of the day, my friend!"

Redbone was startled by the harsh voice of Fast Hawk just before his friend drew the tent flap back and the morning sun blasted him in the face.

"W-what? What is happening? Where am I?" Redbone tried to make sense of what was happening.

"The sun is already above the eastern hills. This is your big trading day, and you are lazing in your blankets like you were struck in the head with a club," Fast Hawk chastised.

"I...I...wa...was up most of the night. I could not sleep, worrying about today..."

"I know, I left the tent so I could get some sleep."

"I went walking up the river trail. Fast Hawk, I found the hidden lodge my mother grew up in, I think. It was just as Mother describes it. Hidden among the rocky ledges east of here. I felt mysteriously tied to the place. It was amazing! I found these." He took the piece of broken pot and the broken arrow shaft from his pack and held them for Fast Hawk to see.

"Yes, very nice. But we need to get moving. I am as starved as a spring bear, and we need to get all your goods out and on display before people start showing up in the plaza to trade."

"You are right, of course. But first, I have personal issues to tend to!" Redbone looked around and learned he had to walk at least ten-tens of paces to get to some screening bushes. He was not sure he could make it that far.

When Redbone and Fast Hawk made their way into the Corn Clan longhouse, they found Corn Silk sitting at the head of the firepit. A bowl that once had corn gruel in it sat next to her chair. She was dressed in a plain brown, loose-fitting dress that had darker brown painted corn ears along the bottom hem that hung about halfway up her calves. The loose dress mostly hid her still slender form. She wore a Corn Clan shell pendant on a plain leather thong around her neck that lay on her chest. She looked like each of her three-tens-and-eight summers had been hard ones. Crow's feet accented her dark eyes and her hair, chopped and sticking out all sides of her head, had only a few black streaks among the dominant gray. Wrinkles surrounded her full lips and curved down her smallish chin. A slender nose hinted at her former beauty. The sagging muscles in her bare arms indicated she was once a powerful woman.

The rest of Corn Silk's family had already gone about their business for the day while Traveler occupied his usual place of honor. His demeanor perked up when the two young men appeared.

"Greetings young traders. Are you prepared for a hard day of vigorous trading?" the elder asked. Corn Silk looked hard at Redbone, ready to judge his answer.

"Ready as ever, Elder. I doubt the trading will take the whole day. My goods are not that plentiful." Then, eyes downcast, he turned to Corn Silk, "We were hoping to get here in time for morning meal, but I overslept."

"You may be lazy, but at least you are honest about it. I think we may have some corn cakes with blueberries still available." She clapped her hands, and a young, plainly dressed maiden came to her side quickly.

"What can I get you, Head Matron?" The girl looked at the floor when she asked.

"I have told you to look at me when speaking to me. I cannot hear you when you talk to the floor. Now, please bring the young warriors what you have left from morning meal and some tea."

"Yes, Head Matron," the girl told the floor matting.

Redbone could hold his tongue no longer. "Traveler, last night I could not sleep. All I could think about was today's trading. Restless, I got up and walked the riverbank toward the rising moon. I followed the river for over a hand of time when I came to a creek. There was an old trail along the creek, so I followed it. At the end of that trail, tucked into the rocky, eroded walls is a pile of logs that burned many sun cycles past. I found some manmade objects among the debris. I think it is the remains of the hermit lodge my mother and aunt lived in. Do you know anything of that place?" His excitement was palpable.

Corn Silk spoke up before Traveler could answer, "No one except Tallow, Water Mint, your mother and aunt, and two of your cousins have even been there. How did you find it in the dark? All signs of it should be erased from the forest by now."

"I do not know, Head Matron. I just happened on it. I was not looking for it. But I found these around there." Redbone took the arrow parts and piece of pottery from his pack to show Corn Silk and Traveler.

"I met with them on a trail, but I never went to their lodge. I cannot say if you found their lodge or not. But that arrow point does look like Cass's work," Traveler added.

"Who is Cass?" Redbone asked, a puzzled look on his face.

"A name that is no longer spoken here!" Corn Silk shot daggers from her eyes at Traveler.

"Sorry, Head Matron. That was a name your aunt used when she lived in that lodge. The name supposedly came to her from First Man. It is connected to the spirit world. The name is not spoken here in deference to whatever spirits cling to it. I should not have spoken it," said Traveler.

"What is done is done. Let us speak no more of this. Eat your cakes and go get on with your trade," Corn Silk ordered Redbone.

"It will be a beautiful day for trading!" Fast Hawk changed the subject, just as the girl brought forth a basket with a few corn cakes. Another girl followed with two cups of steaming tea.

After gobbling down the cakes and slurping their tea, Redbone and Fast Hawk stood and thanked the Head Matron for her hospitality and left for the plaza where they would set up for the trading session.

When they arrived at the central firepit, there were more than two-tens of men standing around waiting. Half that many women were in attendance. Strong Elk and his friend Bear Track joined Redbone and Fast Hawk. Together, they laid out old deer hides to lay out all of Redbone's goods to be displayed. They were almost finished when Traveler wobbled out of the Corn Clan longhouse carrying a heavy looking bag. He brought it over to an empty corner of one of the deer hides.

"You forgot these, Redbone," Traveler called to his young friend and gave him a toothless grin.

"What is in there?" Redbone asked as he took the bag from Traveler.

"See for yourself."

Redbone dropped to his knees and began to empty the bag. The first thing he pulled out was two rabbit skins sewed together. Wrapped in the skins were ten-and-two exquisitely carved Cahokian shell pendants. Each was the size of a spread hand, carved and painted. One featured the Tree of Life growing from Snapping Turtle's back. Another depicted Eagle Man soaring in a blue sky. Still another was a chunky player holding a lance and a chunky stone.

Next, Redbone pulled an otter skin out. In it were two granite chunky stones.

Finally, there was a rabbit skin bag that held two-tens-and-four arrow points.

"Those arrow points were shaped by your aunt Bright Moon," Traveler told the young trader.

Redbone stood with a puzzled look on his face and a tear running down his cheek. "Elder, I cannot take these things. They are yours and far too valuable for the likes of me to be trading."

"Now, Redbone, you are part of my family. I have been hanging onto these trade goods for ten and five sun cycles. I should have sent them with Yellow Hair. I can see now that I was wise to save them for you. I can think of no better trade."

"A...al...right. I will take them. But I will put them back in the bag to use at another trading session. These arrow points I would like to gift to my sister. She sees our aunt as a great hero and will be stunned to get these."

"Wise choice. You show great wisdom. Redbone will be a great trader!"

"Because Redbone chooses to give away valuable trade goods?"

"No! Because Redbone sees the worth of trade goods to his trade partners."

One by one, throughout the morning Redbone began to bargain his goods to the people of Monongahela Village. Midday came and went with people coming around to trade tanned skins for decorated blankets, warclubs for bundles of arrows, chert nodules for finished points and knives, clay pots for deer and elk stomachs, and so on. By midafternoon, every item Redbone had displayed on the deer skins had been exchanged for something of equal or greater value. Though his stomach was growling for lack of food, Redbone was grinning from ear to ear. His first trading session was a huge success.

When the trading was finally finished, Redbone, Fast Hawk, and Strong Elk helped carry the skins and baskets of new items into a storeroom in the Corn Clan longhouse.

The following day, Redbone and Fast Hawk paddled Redbone's canoe up to the creek Redbone had followed to find the burned lodge in the weathered rock wall. By midmorning, they were following the trail along the small creek.

"This trail looks very overgrown. How did you follow it in the dark?" Fast Hawk asked.

"It seemed easier in the dark. The moonlight

accented the contrasting colors better than full sunlight does, I guess," Redbone replied.

"And it was cool that night, and I did not have to deal with all these pesky buzzing and biting insects."

"I am sure glad Strong Elk told us to slather our skin with this bear fat and cedar berries," said Fast Hawk.

"Well, here is where we cross the creek. Maybe they will let up when we get on a little higher ground."

As they climbed the slight incline from the marshy lowland, the mosquitoes did back off some, but that only made more room for the biting flies. But even those voracious bugs slowed down as the young men got closer to the eroded rock wall. Fast Hawk followed Redbone when he turned east at the base of the steep grade. With the separated wall on their left and the steep ridge on their right, the air cooled considerably.

After about fifty steps, Redbone slowed and began searching for more broken arrows. "If I remember the story right, Aunt Bright Moon had slipped and tumbled down from high above. She had hit her head on a tree or rock and was only semicon- scious. Then she slammed to a stop when her back hit a rock. Her otter skin quiver was full of chokecherry arrows. The quiver had slid around and up her back just before she hit the rock. The quiver full of arrows took the brunt of the impact. Supposedly, all her arrows broke, and her quiver was destroyed, but her back was only bruised."

"I would think rolling down that steep hill would break most of my bones. How did she manage?" Fast Hawk asked.

"I never thought to ask, but I think her spirit helper protected her."

"She must have had a powerful spirit helper."

"I think that goes without saying!"

Finally, Redbone found three more broken arrow shafts. The piece where the point would be attached was gone on all three, and the fletching was rotted off each of them. He saw no reason to keep those three half-rotted arrow shafts.

Once that site was thoroughly inspected for more arrows, they moved up the trail. The closer they got to the end of the trail, the darker it became. The sunlight now being blocked from three sides. Just when Fast Hawk was ready to give up and turn around, Redbone declared, "Here we are!"

As they approached the fire-scarred pile of logs, a red-shouldered hawk screamed its scolding call at them for disturbing her quiet hunt. Fast Hawk nearly jumped out of his skin at the screech. If pressed at the moment, he would have confessed that a small amount of urine escaped his bladder. After he calmed down, he studied the tumbled logs and other debris.

"See if you can find anything manmade. I can see some pieces of tanned skins, some even dyed. But where are the things they would have left behind? Things like bed platforms, cooking hearth. There should be at least a couple large, flat rocks, right?" Redbone asked.

"Something is not right here. It just looks odd. Something just looks off. Do you see what I mean?" Fast Hawk asked.

"One that strikes me is that the fire never got very hot. It seem the logs that are fire-scarred should have burned to a small pile of ash. Probable weathered away by now. That was what, ten and five or six sun cycles past? I wonder if they got the fire started, left, and then it started raining and put the fire out," Redbone speculated.

"Good point. Surely Water Mint should remember that," Fast Hawk declared.

"I just have a feeling there is something here I am missing. I think we can move some of these logs to get at whatever is underneath. Come and help me."

The logs were twined together like a twist of sweetgrass traders sometimes brought from the west. They were finally able to pull one from the top. That made it easier to get the next one loose and pulled out of the way. As they worked, the problem became what to do with the logs they were pulling loose. In the confined area between the rock walls, there was little space to move the debris out of their way. They were about to give up when Fast Hawk heaved the butt end of a log away from the center of the pile. The sun, which was now overhead, shone light into a large cavity.

"Look! It opens up into a room. It is badly charred, but it looks stable. I think I can drop down there. It cannot be more than shoulder deep." Fast Hawk excitedly pointed down into the gap between logs he had opened.

"Let me go first. This was my family's home," Redbone demanded.

"Of course. I will wait until you think it is safe for both of us to go in there," Fast Hawk replied.

"Ouch!" Redbone exclaimed when he dropped into the cavernous room below. "Something hard on the floor jabbed into my foot."

He carefully dropped to his knees and examined his right moccasin for damage. There was none, but his foot still throbbed. Then he slid his hand across the floor. It was packed ash, but suddenly his hand ran into something hard. Using his fingers, he dug around the hard object. Soon he had enough exposed to see it was a stone shaped in the form of a dog or a wolf. More digging, and he had it freed from the ash bed. Just below the carving was bare dirt. There was just over a finger-deep layer of ash on the floor.

Looking closer at the wolf, he could see it was well made and chipped from a hard stone, maybe chert. It was hard to tell because it was charred beyond Redbone's recognition. After dusting as much of the ash off as he could, he slipped it into his shoulder pack.

It could belong to any of them, but since it is obviously a wolf, I suspect it was Aunt Bright Moon's. Mother will be delighted to see it again.

"Now that you are finished playing with toys, what do you see down there?" Fast Hawk demanded.

Redbone looked around. Most of the room was in dark shadow, with a bright column of sunlight streaming into the hole they had opened. He could make out the charred framework of the lodge, even a few remnants of the burned and rotted hides that covered the frame. One corner was obviously caved in, and the rest was being held up by the entangled logs on the outside.

"It looks as if the old lodge is ready to collapse at any moment. I think I should get out of here while I can. It looks like everything in here burned except that stone wolf. Give me a hand, I am coming up."

Redbone reached up for Fast Hawk's strong arm. Redbone wriggled out of the hole. Once on his feet, the sound of cracking wood emanated from the hole, and the young men felt their support giving way. Both scrambled to the west side where they had piled the logs they had pulled loose. The domed room collapsed into a cloud of old ash and dust, shooting a geyser of it up through the hole they had created. They had barely made it onto the log pile when the rest of the tangled debris cascaded down on itself.

Precariously hanging on to a log, Fast Hawk

declared, "I think we are finished looking in the old lodge now."

"So it would seem. I am glad I decided to get out when I did. Do you want to explore some more?" asked Redbone.

"No, I am ready to leave. But let us eat those corn cakes and some jerky here. The bugs will give us too much help with our food if we wait until we are down in the lowlands."

"Good idea!"

They scrambled off the unsteady log pile and moved to some more secure rocks. While they were sitting on the rocks relaxing as they ate, Redbone asked, "Are you wanting to get home? I would not mind seeing Mother and Father, even Sister."

"Well, I am more interested in seeing Green Lark, to be honest. Dancing with her is more appealing than arguing with Father about how long I have been gone," Fast Hawk replied.

"Ha! I can see what you mean. But I do not have a Green Lark to hold me here. And Traveler seems much stronger than when we arrived. I think it did him some good to have us 'pesky children' under foot. The many conversations about trading reawakened his life soul, I think. I believe he will be waiting for me to return from the Lenape lands."

"Yes. Almost a miraculous difference in him. I thought for sure he would follow his wife on the Path of the Ancestors. Your enthusiasm for the trade rubbed off on him!"

"So, do you think there is something permanent with you and Green Lark? Her parents seem to like you."

"I would like to think so, but that Wolf Clan warrior, Hunting Fox, is pushing her, too. He is bigger than me and has a whole tongue. He can say words better that I can. We will see."

"He may be bigger and can talk clearly, but he cannot come close to your charm. I bet on you. Let us head down river. It will be late afternoon before we get back now."

Two days later, Redbone was on the Ohi-yo River, paddling north. He was alone. Fast Hawk decided if he was going to sway Green Lark away from Hunting Fox, he would need to be there. He had been welcomed into the Hawk Clan longhouse and could stay there as long as he needed.

Redbone found the trip upriver much more strenuous and the currents more difficult to read. But he soon got comfortable and learned his bark canoe was easier to navigate that the dugouts in those currents. He was happy with his whole Monongahela undertaking. Having Traveler feeling stronger was a great relief, even though he knew in his heart his elder friend's health could falter at any time.

CHAPTER 9
HOME

By midday, the landing at New Long Pine Village came into view. After six days on the river, Redbone would be back in his home. He looked forward to sharing the things that had happened in Monongahela Village after they had returned following the Summer Solstice Celebration.

Two canoes with five young warriors met him and escorted him the last hand of time as he approached the landing. He would have plenty of help carrying his packs, bags, and baskets up the hill and into the village.

"Greetings, Redbone! Did you finally remember how to get back home? And what have you done with my brother?" asked Silver Hawk, Fast Hawk's older brother, as the first canoe pulled alongside his.

"I have my reasons for staying that long in Monongahela Village. And Fast Hawk has his reasons for staying longer."

"He probably could not wake up in time, so you had to leave him behind," sniped Long Nose, a young warrior of the Wolf Clan.

Redbone rolled his eyes but did not respond. He remained silent as he guided his canoe toward an open slot at the landing. When his laden canoe slid to a stop, he stepped out as gracefully on his clubbed foot as those with normal feet. None noticed the normal things he did but were quick to point out his awkward movements due to his deformed foot.

Despite the odd disparaging comment, all the young men pitched in to help carry his cargo up the hill and to the Water Plant longhouse. Not helping the son of the Head Matron would be a mistake, no matter how odd that son seemed.

The first person to greet him when he stepped into the dim light within the Head Matron's lodge was his sister, Bright Moon. She loudly welcomed him home and gave him a big hug. He realized how much he missed her and hugged her just as hard.

His mother was next in line and added a kiss on the cheek to her hug. He was surprised when his father clasped him in a breath-robbing bear hug.

"You do not look any worse for the wear. It looks as if Corn Silk has been feeding you," Bright Star quipped.

"She has. And the meat in the Corn Clan longhouse has been provided by Strong Elk and Redbone. I have many things to tell you," Redbone answered.

Then added, "Everything here looks normal and quiet."

"I killed a moose this morning, and only used one arrow!" Bright Moon bragged. "We were just getting ready to eat some backstrap for a midday meal. Tonight, we will feast!"

"Good, I am famished," Redbone replied.

"Come sit, my son. You can tell your stories while we eat some of your sister's moose," said Bright Star.

Everyone, including the children, around the firepit had chopped their hair in mourning for the Head Matron who had passed. All worn leather headbands to keep the uneven, unruly hair from their faces. They were dressed in varying everyday attire featuring buckskin, doeskin, or woven fabric shirts, vests, leggings, or dresses. All sported some sort of clan decorations, but none were showy.

"All right. After all of you left, Strong Elk and I went out and killed a deer. Traveler asked me to bring him some fresh liver because chewing meat is too hard for him with his teeth mostly gone now. Well, you should see the difference in him after eating that fresh liver. He seems twenty sun cycles younger.

"In the plaza that evening, he had Red Oak announce that the next day, there would be a trade session featuring my trade goods. I was astonished. Strangers started asking what sorts of things I had to trade."

"That must have made you feel good," Red Hand offered.

"It did! But I was so nervous about the trade, I could not even close my eyes. Fast Hawk left the tent because I was keeping him awake. Finally, I gave up and went for a walk along the river bank trail. I randomly followed the river upstream. The stars and moon lit the trail enough to easily follow it.

"Ater a while, I came to a creek that blocked the trail. Then I could see a trail leading to the south, along the creekbank."

Tallow, Water Mint, and Bright Star exchanged glances.

"I followed that trail a ways, It was somewhat overgrown, but still, I could pick my way along it. I felt like something was drawing me along. Eventually, the trail crossed the creek and began to climb. Soon I came to a place where part of the rock hillside had split away from the ridge. The trail split, but for no reason, I turned east along the base of the steep ridge. Soon, I noticed something bright just up the slope from the leaf-packed trail."

He reached into his pack and pulled out the broken arrow shaft and arrow point. Bright Star put the back of her hand to her mouth and gasped. She knew that arrow. Tears leaked from her eyes.

Tears filled Water Mint's eyes. "I...I remember that night," she said, barely a whisper. Her eyes unfocused as she looked into the past.

"Sounds like you have a story to tell—about Redbone's story!" Bright Moon blurted out excitedly.

"I am sorry. I should not interrupt. Please continue, Redbone," Water Mint quietly said as she wiped the tears from her face and eyes.

"As you can see, I picked up the broken arrow and brought it for all of you to see. This arrow point means a lot to many of you. I will let you decide what to do with it. The shaft is half rotted and very delicate. Handle it with care."

He passed the broken arrow to his mother. She studied it closely through watery eyes before handing it to Water Mint without saying a word.

Water Mint looked at it briefly, then drifted back into the past as she handed it to Tallow. He smiled as he examined it closely.

"By the time she made this point, she was a better flint-knapper than me. And I taught her how! She did everything better." Tallow spoke to everyone and no one, wistful awe in his deep voice.

"Redbone has another surprise for all of you," said Redbone.

"What is it?" eight voices chimed in. The ninth voice only said, "Waa!" Hopper, Water Mint's three-summers-old son was confused by every was looking at things he was not allowed to touch while they smiled, laughed, and cried. Often at the same time.

Redbone reached into his bag, making a dramatic show of bringing the object out without letting anyone see it. Then, he made them all close their eyes, held the stone wolf carving out, and announced, "Everyone open your eyes!"

The room was filled with an audible gasp.

"Where did you get that?" Bright Star demanded as more tears flooded from her eyes.

"Two days after my trading session, Fast Hawk and I went back to the log pile to see if we could find anything you may have left behind. We were amazed that, despite the fire, most of the logs were little more than scorched. We could only conclude that it must have rained before the logs were consumed by the flames."

"Yes, that is exactly what happened. We got soaked going down the river. I never went back to see what had happened."

"We searched throughout the lodge for that wolf and concluded that Ca...Bright Moon took it with her when she went on her war walk. She said it was a connection to Wolf, First Man," Tallow explained.

"When I dropped down through the hole in the roof that Fast Hawk and I had opened up, I felt a sharp jab in my right foot. All I could see on the floor was a layer of packed ash and dust. I felt around in the ash with my hands until I found something hard. It took several heartbeats to dig this out of the ash and dirt. It was mostly buried in the dirt floor. I assume you had mat coverings on the floor?" Redbone asked rhetorically.

"Yes." Bright Star's voice was barely a whisper. Her sobs almost drowned her reply.

"She chipped that wolf likeness from white quartz when she had seen ten and five summers—just about your age. She was a skilled stone worker by then. The effigy was pure white when she made it, but it looks as though it was scorched in the fire," Tallow offered. "Could you tell where it was located in the lodge?"

"It appeared that everything in the interior was consumed by the flames. I could not even tell where the hearth had been. There was a shaft of bright light streaming through the hole we opened, but the light was dim everywhere else."

"The lodge was constructed so that those logs you were moving around supported the roof poles from the outside," Tallow added.

"Right after I put the wolf into my pack, I heard several of the roof poles crack. I had Fast Hawk help me out of there, and we barely got away from the hole when the entire roof collapsed. It raised a great choking cloud of dust and ash. When the dust settled, we were filthy. Luckily we managed to scramble over the logs and away from the cave-in.

"While we caught our breath, we ate some jerky and corn cakes, then started down the trail back to our canoe. We spent some time at the creek washing our clothes and bodies. It was late afternoon when we returned to Monongahela Village.

"Do you want to tell your story now, Aunt Water Mint?" Redbone wanted to let someone else talk.

"If everyone wants to hear it. I may get emotional

telling it." Water Mint looked at each of the family members around the firepit.

"Hopper want feed," the youngest member of the family said as he climbed onto Water Mint's lap and searched for access to her breast. She opened her loose-fitting shirt and let him suckle before starting her story.

"Bright Star was on one of her monthly *hunts*." She looked at Red Hand and winked, "and Bright Moon stayed to help me with the children. That was out of character for her because she would rather hunt than breathe in those days. I think she just did not want to get in the way between Bright Star and Red Hand." Water Mint watched Red Hand look at the fire while Bright Star looked at her hands through watery eyes as her face turned crimson.

"By the third morning, Bright Moon was so bored she could not sit still. Finally, she grabbed her bow and said she was going hunting. Said she would be back by sunset. It was in the Awakening Moon, I believe.

"I was busy with the children and did not notice the time passing. It had been a warm morning and afternoon. Then, just before sunset, a cold rain blew in from the northwest. As dark descended, it got cold, and the rain changed to a freezing mist.

"I began to worry about Bright Moon. Her mind was not on her task. I could tell because she did not take her normal gear with her, and she was not dressed for cold rain. Darkness fell, and she was still out there in the forest, alone. Normally, I knew she could take care of herself in any circumstance, but she was just not herself that day. With the children here, I could not go search for her, and Tallow had duties in Monongahela Village. I could only wait.

"I fixed a venison stew for evening meal. When she did not show up by dark, and that rain coming down, I knew she was in trouble. I managed to get the children to sleep, but I lay in my sleeping skins and worried."

"I curse myself for letting the beloved Head Matron coerce me to spend so much time away from you and the children," Tallow offered.

"You had little choice, my husband. It was that, or she would send warriors out to scour this forest and bring us back as prisoners. No one blames you for doing your duty.

"Well, deep into the night, I hear noises outside. I jumped up and put fresh wood in the firepit for warmth and for light. At last, Bright Moon stumbled through the door hanging.

"She was a mess! Her hair was wet and filled with sticks, leaves, mud, and blood. Her clothes were soaked and clung to her like a second skin. Her moccasins were hard to see for all the mud, leaves, and sticks clinging to them. She was frozen, and all her movements were awkward, something I had not seen since she was a toddler like this one." She pointed to Hopper, who was fast asleep on her lap.

"I had to cut her clothes off her because she could

not move, nor did she have the strength to help. Once I got her stripped down, I wrapped her in a warm elk skin, and she slowly began to warm up. When she was able to start talking, she told me how she let herself get distracted at the wrong time, how the bear attacked her, and how she managed her escape.

"By then, it was a pitch-black night, and she was off any trail she knew. Her feet were cold, so she just stumbled around. Finally, she found the top of the ridge above us, but she stumbled when she started down. She ended up sliding and tumbling down the steep grade until her back slammed into a rock at the base.

"Somehow, her quiver, which was full of arrows, ended up between her back and the rock. The breaking arrows cushioned the impact, so she was not seriously injured. But she did get a nasty gash just above her hairline over her left eye. That was where all the blood came from. She discovered her bow had also been broken in the fall.

"By some grace of the forest spirits, when she pulled herself to her feet, she could smell my stew simmering by the fire, along with smoke. She followed the scent to our door hanging. I was still awake and could hear her stumbling outside the door opening.

"That is my story of how that broken arrow ended up where Redbone found it. When Bright

Moon felt strong enough, she went back and found her bow and most of the arrows. It looks like she missed one.

"Tallow, you remember coming home and seeing the disturbed mud and leaves on the trail?" Water Mint asked her husband.

"Of course. I could not miss that mess. I thought Bright Moon had killed a deer on the ridge that slid down the hill and ended up right there. When I learned the real story, it was even more incredible!"

"Can we get started on evening meal, now? I am hungry and tired of old stories," six-summers-old Morning asked.

"Yes, I think we have been sitting for long enough," Water Mint said, as they all stiffly rose from their places at the firepit.

"Sister, Mother, Aunt, I have one more pack I wish to share with you. I agree, we have been sitting long enough. I can show you these things while we stand, if you do not mind," Redbone said to his female relatives.

"What do you have, brother?" Bright Moon, now ten-and-four-summers-old asked. She was dressed more like a warrior than the pretty maiden her face and body displayed. Her hair was chopped in mourning like everyone else's.

"A few things Traveler gave me that you may be interested in."

Redbone pulled a coyote skin bag from his

shoulder pack that appeared to be heavy. He set it on the floor and pulled out a rabbit skin pouch first. Then he handed the pouch to Bright Moon, who juggled it like she was trying to judge what was in it.

"See what is in there." He pointed to the thong that tied the bag closed.

Half looking at him, she untied the thong and reached into the bag. She pulled out a triangular arrow point that looked exceptionally well made. Holding that one with her little finger, she took another out. It was the same high quality shaped point made of a gray-colored flint. She looked at her mother, aunt, and finally back to Redbone with curiosity in her eyes.

"There are two-tens-and-four arrow points in that bag. They are made from different colored flint from the western mountains. But mainly they were made by Aunt Bright Moon. Traveler kept them when they left him behind on their journey to Yellow Hair's lands. Traveler decided it was foolish to hang on to them any longer. He gave them to me for my trade, but I think they are better suited to fill your quiver than some strange warrior's." Redbone put his hand on Bright Moon's shoulder.

Bright Moon looked at the arrow points in awe. Bright Star and Water Mint were struggling to hold back their tears. All were speechless.

Tallow and Red Hand were closely watching the exchange. They both smiled and remained quiet while their women shared the emotional exchange silently.

Finally, Bright Moon looked up at her brother and spoke in a quiet voice, "I know not what to say, Brother. I am honored that you trust me with this family treasure, but..." She broke into sobs as she put the two points in the bag and hugged it to her chest. Tears let loose and flowed down her cheeks. Bright Star and Water Mint stepped close and hugged Bright Moon while all three cried together.

"There is more!" exclaimed Redbone.

He pulled another rabbit skin from his pack and dumped several sharpened stone items onto the floor mat. "There are five lance points, ten women's knives, seven scrapers, five awls, and a smaller bag that contains seven drills of varying sizes, including two fine enough to drill holes in small beads. Traveler said these were all made by Bright Moon from blanks she traded for in Cahokia. She made the points in her spare time while they were in various camps on their way from Cahokia to Monongahela Village. Then she gave them all to Traveler for everything he had done for her and Yellow Hair. He was responsible for bringing them together, if you recall. You can decide what to do with these things. I thought you should have them. I have no more surprises."

Bright Moon stepped over to Redbone and hugged him tight.

"Thank you, Brother. You have no idea how much this means to me." He felt her hot, wet tears on his neck.

"We all thank you, son. And now, we should eat!" Bright Moon added.

CHAPTER 10

TRADE ROUTE

R edbone was beside himself with excitement as he, Water Racer, and Blue Deer shoved off from the New Long Pine Village canoe landing. It was late in the Planting Moon, and spring floodwaters had receded to manageable levels. They would travel downriver to the Kiskiminetas River. From there, they would follow that river to its headwaters, then follow a series of portages and smaller rivers until they hit the headwaters of the Juniata. They would follow it to the Mud River, then to Blue Crab Village.

Blue Deer and Water Racer were well acquainted with the trail, so Redbone took his place in the middle of the canoe and followed Blue Deer's instructions. There were many rapids and areas of low water on the Kiskiminetas which required a number of portages. In many cases, they could simply get out and pull the craft through the shallow areas until they were in deep enough water to float. On some occasions, they had to carry their packs, bags, and baskets past waters that were not navigable. The farther they moved into the headwaters, the more frequent the portages were. Although Redbone felt himself getting stronger day by day, he was worried his club foot would slow them down, but he received no complaints.

They encountered several individual farmsteads and a few clusters of dwellings unaffiliated with the Monongahela nation or any clans. They managed a few trades, but those small families had little to part with and were completely self-sufficient in their little clusters. Almost all of them were familiar and friendly with Blue Deer and Water Racer. Redbone found them to be friendly to him as well. For the most part, they all wanted news of the world outside their little family groups. Most were more than happy to trade sumptuous meals for stories. Redbone was surprised to hear that all of them had heard about the death of the former Head Matron of the Monongahela nation.

Redbone was glad when they finally started working their way downhill toward the rising sun. The final portage from the Kiskiminetas drainage was the longest and most strenuous so far. He was happy when a navigable stretch of water came into view. By the time they had covered the winding trail three times carrying the dugout and all of their packs and gear, the trio was ready to make camp in the evening twilight. Their first trek had begun before the sun rose in the east.

The going was slow along the headwaters of the Juniata due to the intermittent nature of the upper river. They did get lucky when a heavy rain raised the water level enough for them to float for two full days between portages on one stretch. As they descended from the highlands, they ran into more farmsteads and some small villages. The terrain made growing the three sisters difficult. As a result, the population remained low. The farmers present were not interested in aligning with any nations that would require them to pay a tribute.

Finally, the Juniata opened up with a wider channel and steady flow. One day, they approached a bend in the river with a creek flowing in from the north. They made camp on that little creek. They had a good fire going and three fat ducks to roast. Ducks were plentiful along the river, with many nesting pairs. Duck eggs were easy to collect and were a welcome addition to any meal.

"This is where we camped when Yellow Hair set up our defenses to fight off an attack by an aggressive Haudenosaunee war chief," Blue Deer began his story. "The river follows around that hill just over there." He pointed downriver to the hill on the north side of the channel.

"That hill slopes down to a drop-off along the river. The water is deep along that side. Yellow Hair had all of us, including his wife who was heavy with child, set up within bow range just above that cut bank. He told us to wound as many as we could in each canoe. With nowhere to put ashore on this side, the enemy would be forced to flee to the south bank. Their wounded would need to be tended to. Yellow Hair wounded their war chief, and as he guessed, they fled downriver to find someplace to help their wounded. But they were in Lenape lands and had to make their way all the way back to Mud Town, which had been renamed Ganeco Village after the war chief. That gave us the opportunity to flee up the Mud River and over to Sun Town.

"Yellow Hair's plan was brilliant. None of us got even a scratch while ten-and-six of his four-tens of warriors were wounded. I do not know of the others but learned that the war chief was invaded by evil spirits from his leg wound and died. There was much rejoicing in the Lenape lands after that. There was no one as capable as him to take his place. To this day, they are causing little trouble, and I have even been able to trade in some of their villages."

Redbone hung on every word, committing them to memory. *I may be trading with those people in the coming days. I need to learn everything I can about them.*

"Do you see more problems from the Haudenosaunee in the future?" Redbone asked Blue Deer.

"I think it depends on their chief. Some seem content with their territory and are peaceful. Others are bent on taking slaves and adding to their territories. The northern traders say the Haudenosaunee bands to the north are always fighting one another. As long as they are fighting among themselves, they are leaving others alone."

"I have heard that the Lenape fight among themselves, as well."

"Some, but not like the Haudenosaunee. Among the Lenape, there are northern bands who have little contact with their southern neighbors. In the local lands, the Crab Bay Lenape want to control the river bands so they can control the trade coming along the coast and from the west. It is all about greed. I try to stay neutral and trade with them all."

"Sounds like a good plan," Redbone offered.

"I hear tell that since the Fort Ancient peoples have declined, the trade from the west has been more difficult to get. The Illini peoples are supposedly interrupting goods coming from the Grandfather River, and fewer goods are coming through. Is that true?" Blue Deer asked.

"That is what Traveler tells me. I plan to attempt to get to Cahokia and back in the future. I hope the troubles end, and we can all benefit."

"Good thinking. I think our duck stew is done now. What say we eat, and get some sleep?" Water Racer cut in.

"One more question—will we get to Blue Crab Village tomorrow?" Redbone asked.

"A few more days, I hope! I pray Spring Flower is still waiting for me," Water Racer exclaimed.

"It will be at least late afternoon three days later, depending on how long we stay in Ottertail Village. The werowance, or chief, there will not let us just pass by," said Blue Deer.

"I forgot about Red Bear. He thinks everyone else's business is his business," Water Racer added.

"Yes, their werowanskua, or Head Matron, does little to keep him under control."

"What about you, Redbone? Do you have a young maiden waiting for you anywhere?" Blue Deer asked.

"No. I have not looked for one. With this crippled foot, what maiden would want me? They always want a strong warrior to take care of them. I am no warrior."

"Ha! Do not sell yourself short, my friend. You are a good provider, and you have access to exotic trade goods, which also lures the maidens," Blue Deer quickly pointed out.

"And, as traders, we are not home long enough to make a maiden happy, or to keep them from seeking other company," Redbone answered.

"That is my worry," Water Racer added.

"Tanager has never strayed on me, and she is always happy when I return. I think it is a matter of finding the right maiden," said Blue Deer.

"Easy to say for one who has found the right one.

I have never even seen one looking at me with longing in her eyes. I think my fate is a long life of celibacy," Redbone quipped.

"No, do not say that, Redbone. The next maiden you meet may be the one. Always keep your eyes open," Water Racer joined in.

"I noted that you kept your eyes and your breech-clout open while you were in Monongahela Village last summer," Redbone chided the young man.

"Well, a man has needs, and when a chance to... you know."

"And does Spring Flower agree that you should tend to your needs while she waits for you to return to tend to her own needs?"

"That is a woman's duty," Water Racer replied confidently.

"Red Hand says that attitude is why so many men find their belongings outside their ex-wife's lodge when they finally get home," Redbone added.

"It is the woman's duty to wait for the man, and the man must tend to his needs if he is to remain vigilant and ready for battle."

Blue Deer leaned forward and took a burning twig from the fire and lit his clay pipe. As a cloud of blue smoke billowed around his head, he leaned back against a cottonwood, enjoying the banter between his young followers.

By the time the eastern sky turned orange with the beginning of a new day, the trio was on the water approaching the confluence of the Juniata and Mud

Rivers. They would make Ottertail Village before midday.

Shortly after they joined the flow of the Mud River, four canoes with four warriors each joined them.

"You have not been gone long enough to do any trading. What have you been up to, trader? And who is this one with the odd cut to his clothes?" a big warrior demanded.

Redbone understood precious few of the man's words.

"We were not trading. We went west to the Ohi-yo River, as it is now called. We went there to get this young trader who will learn from me before he sets out on his own," Blue Deer replied.

"How long will you remain as our guests, eating our food?" the burly warrior asked.

"We will be gone as soon as Dancing Bear permits."

"Good!"

A short trading session the morning after they arrived at Ottertail Village, and the trio pushed off from the canoe landing. It took three days to reach Blue Crab Village at the mouth of the Mud River.

As soon as word spread around the sprawling village that was not confined by a palisade, people began to gather at the canoe landing to hear any news the traders might bring and to see what goods they had to offer.

Among the throngs of people gathered, Water Racer spied Spring Flower. The petite maiden, wearing a doeskin dress with Turtle Clan symbols painted in the four sacred colors, and similar moccasins, stood with a broad smile across her round face. Her hair was plaited into a pair of braids hanging down her back, indicating she was not married. She had seen ten-and-four-summers. He rushed to her, and they embraced without kissing. The young couple talked for several heartbeats.

"When you push off for Lenape Town, Water Racer will be staying in Blue Crab Village," Water Racer proudly announced.

"When is the wedding?" Blue Deer asked.

"I do not know yet, but Spring Flower says it will be soon. She missed her moon, and her mother says she will have us married before her belly begins to grow. Water Racer will be a father!"

"If not on the rivers trading, how will you provide for your family?" Redbone asked. His Lenape tongue was much improved.

"My bow is strong, and my arrows are sharp. I can hunt and clear fields just like most others do."

"I think you will miss the rivers, but that is your choice," Blue Deer added.

Two mornings later, Redbone and Blue Deer shoved off for Lenape Town. The days were rapidly warming. Most days they slathered their bodies with bear grease and mint, wearing only breechclouts and moccasins. By late afternoon on the second day, they could see the smoke rising from the many cooking fires in Lenape Town.

Tanager was among the many people that welcomed them at the canoe landing. She looked at Redbone and said, "I can see you are not Water Racer, so you must be Redbone. Welcome to Lenape Town, and I hope you are well."

"Tanager, meet Redbone of the Water Plant Clan of the lineage of Bright Moon, Head Matron of New Long Pine Village on the Ohi-yo River. Redbone, meet Tanager, wife of Blue Deer. She is Turkey Clan of the lineage of Big Hen, Head Matron of the Turkey Clan of the Turkey People of Lenape Town on the Lenape River.

"Redbone is honored to meet Tanager. I have heard much about Tanager, all of it good, Matron." Redbone offered his right hand, palm up and fingers extended.

"Always an honor to meet a stranger with such good manners and who has made the effort to learn the tongue spoken in this village." She took his fingertips and nodded her approval.

Blue Deer told some young men that had gathered around Blue Deer's canoe to carry their packs to Blue Deer's lodge in the Turkey Clan cluster of longhouses and lodges.

"Now, what you need, husband, is a bath and a sweat before we go to my mother's longhouse," Tanager announced as they approached Tanager's large single-family lodge.

Her lodge was bigger than other single-family dwellings because it served as a storehouse for Blue Deer's trade goods. He had certain goods that he traded to the south around Great Crab Bay and others he traded along the rivers to the north. Most goods overlapped, of course, but he had learned what was most in demand in the different regions of the Lenape lands.

Blue Deer and Redbone spent several days getting acquainted with the peoples, clans, and leaders of Lenape Town. Redbone was well received and his goods traded well. He was, once again, disappointed that no attractive maidens paid him much attention. After ten-and-two days in Lenape Town, they struck out for Willet Village.

"The Solstice Celebration is to be held in Willet Village for all the river Lenni Lenape villages this sun cycle. We should have good trades and meet many important people from the Lenape nation. The river peoples have three people: the Turtle People, the Turkey People, and the Wolf People. Each of the Peoples have their respective clans. I am not sure all the villages will be represented, but the three peoples will be represented, along with most of their clans. I have been told that Willet Village has always hosted a well-attended Solstice Celebration."

"How many people do you expect to be there?" Redbone asked.

"I cannot say with any confidence, but it will rival Lenape Town during the Celebration."

"So, if we trade with everyone at Willet Village, will it be necessary to visit all the other along the rivers?"

"Let us see how we do in Willet Village before we decide."

"Sounds like a plan," Redbone replied.

CHAPTER 11
WILLET VILLAGE

By midday on their second full day on the Mullica River, they began to overtake canoes going to Willet Village for the Solstice Celebration. Redbone had wanted to visit Willet Village because that is where Yellow Hair washed ashore. He hoped to find someone who had known the boy when he first arrived.

"Greetings, Strong Wing," Blue Deer addressed a powerful warrior paddling a large canoe with a Matron, two maidens, and a young man who was paddling from the front of the vessel. Seven other canoes were just in front of that one, all moving downriver.

The warrior looked over his shoulder, smiled, and greeted Blue Deer. "Come to clean out all the clans attending the Solstice Celebration, trader?" Strong Wing addressed Blue Deer with a broad smile.

"We thought we would see what we could swindle out of you river farmers," Blue Deer replied.

"That figures. I do not believe I know your partner there. Did Water Racer tire of your company?" Strong Wing asked.

"In a manner of speaking. He found a young maiden he could not live without and stayed in Blue Crab Village."

"No one could fault him for that!"

By now everyone in three canoes had stopped paddling, gathered, and were listening to their deputy war chief and the trader bantering.

"My friend, here, is Redbone from the Monongahela lands west of the mountains," Blue Deer stated.

"Are you lost, Redbone?" Strong Wing asked.

"No. I am learning the trade with Blue Deer before I set out for the Grandfather River," Redbone replied.

"Plenty ambitious, I wish you well. Why did you come east first?" Strong Wing asked.

"I was in Monongahela Village to see Traveler..."

"Traveler? He still breathes?"

"For now. He is old and feeble, but he likes to talk trading with me. How do you know him?"

"Did he tell you the story of Yellow Hair?"

"Yes! Yellow Hair is the reason I wanted to come to Willet Village. I would like to find someone who knew him when he first came to these lands."

"That would be me. I was there when we found

him, half dead on the beach. I would be happy to take you out there and show you where."

"I would be grateful the rest of my days!" Redbone was so excited he could hardly contain himself.

"We have much to talk about and should put our paddles in the water and get to Willet Village then," Strong Wing suggested. All the canoes picked up the pace as they moved east down the river.

Two hands of time before dark they could see smoke rising above the trees on the north side of the river. Redbone had to restrain himself to stay in line with the eight canoes in front of them. Finally, they passed a point, and a large meadow came into view. The edges of the meadow were a flurry of activity as different villages and clans claimed their campsites.

A large woman directed the Sun Town contingent to a place along the river close to the palisade of the village and a short distance up a creek that flowed into the river. As soon as she was ashore, the large woman began directing clans and families where to set up their temporary homes. She was obviously the Sakimaxkwe and fully in charge. No one questioned her authority.

When the camp was all set up, Strong Wing brought Blue Deer and Redbone over to the Great Sakimaxkwe. Willow Branch, wife of Strong Wing and daughter of the Great Sakimaxkwe, began the introductions.

"Great Sakimaxkwe Round Shell, allow me to

introduce our guests. You are acquainted with the trader, Blue Deer. His new apprentice is Redbone, son of Bright Star of the Yellow Lotus Lineage of the Water Plant Clan and Head Matron of New Long Pine Village in the Monongahela Nation. Redbone is interested in finding all he can from us about Yellow Hair." Willow Branch indicated Redbone as she talked.

"Greetings, young trader. Does that crippled foot hinder your ability to trade on the rivers? I think it would slow you down too much to be of any use." Round Shell had immediately noticed Redbone's deformed foot.

"Greetings, Great Sakimaxkwe. No, it does not hinder me in the trade, but it slows me down too much to be of use in battle. I suppose that is why I took up the trade."

"You have good command of our tongue. Did Blue Deer teach you?"

"Yes, Great Sakimaxkwe."

"Did Strong Wing tell you he knew Yellow Hair? I will let him tell you what he knows. I never really trusted him," Round Shell said with no feeling.

"Strong Wing said he would take me to the place where he found him on the beach."

"Well, do not expect anything. Surely all evidence has washed away sun cycles past."

"Redbone understands, Great Sakimaxkwe," Redbone replied.

"We should go into the village and introduce Redbone to Red Feather," Willow Branch suggested.

"Yes. Go ahead. I will be along presently," Round Shell said.

She is a strange one. Not very friendly. Redbone kept his thoughts to himself.

"Children, make yourselves useful around camp. Your father and I are going to take Redbone and Blue Deer into the village to meet the Sakimaxkwe," Willow Branch ordered her children.

"I want to come," Red Petal said. She was much more interested in seeing Hawkeye than Red Feather. Hawkeye was Red Feather's youngest son and had seen two-tens of sun cycles. Red Petal was ten-and-eight sun cycles-old. She did not see him as her uncle because he was close to her age, and Willet Village was so far from Sun Town. But he was strong and handsome. Being her father's brother did not deaden her attraction to him.

"Girl, how many times must I tell you, a relationship with Hawkeye is incest-forbidden by all nations," Willow Branch admonished her oldest daughter.

"Oh Mother, Hawkeye and Red Petal are friends and cousins. We know that. We just like to talk, you know, like cousins do."

"See that all you do is talk. Come on, then." Willow Branch could never say "no" to her beautiful daughter.

The group of five made their way through the

palisade and saw Red Feather sitting near the plaza firepit talking to some other matrons.

"Greetings, daughter-in-law. I know Blue Deer, but who is this with the strange cut and clan symbols on his clothing?" Red Feather said to Willow Branch. She wore a yellow doeskin dress with Turkey Clan embroidered bead turkey tracks, spirals, and chevrons. Her gray-streaked hair was worn in a bun at the back of her head and secured with bone hairpins. A red-tailed hawk tail feather hung down from the base of her bun. The warm evening was comfortable on her bare arms. Her four-tens-and-five sun cycles shown only in the crow's feet at the corners of her eyes and mouth. Her teeth were still white and straight in her mouth. She was still a beauty.

"Sakimaxkwe Red Feather, please allow me to introduce Redbone, son of Bright Star of the Yellow Lotus lineage of the Water Plant Clan and Head Matron of New Long Pine Village in the Monongahela Nation," Willow Branch recited.

Red Feather looked close at Redbone, evaluating him. He felt like a mouse in the shadow of a circling hawk.

"Hmm, Monongahela, you say? I recall a trader who talked much about a matron in that nation," Red Feather mused.

"An honor to greet you, Sakimaxkwe Red Feather," said Redbone. "I am in your presence because of that trader. Traveler still draws air, though he is old and feeble. He talks highly of his time in Willet Village."

"He is a good man as I recall. He was here looking for *Tuh*, who was taken from us by the Great Saki-maxkwe in Sun Town and renamed Yellow Hair when he became a man. Traveler was duty bound to deliver Yellow Hair to some great chief in Cahokia as I recall."

"All you say is correct, Sakimaxkwe. I never met Yellow Hair, but he is my uncle. He is married to my aunt, but they found a way to travel across the Great Ocean to lands of his people, and they have never returned."

"That is the story I recall. But you say Traveler is still alive?"

"Yes, I have tried to spend time and learn all I can from him. I dream of becoming a great river trader like him. I seem to have a special bond with him. He enjoys telling me about the trade and his long life."

A tear trickled down her cheek.

"I became good friends with him when he was hunting for Yellow Hair. He is cunning and knowl-edgeable. Where is he living?" Bear Claw asked.

"Forgive me, Redbone! I did not introduce you to my husband. Redbone, meet Bear Claw, War Chief of Willet Village, of the Mother Bear lineage of the Bear Clan of the Wolf People of Sun Town and married to Red Feather, Sakimaxkwe of Willet Village," said Red Feather.

"It is my honor to meet you, War Chief Bear Claw," Redbone said.

"I plan to take Redbone out to the beach where we found 'Tuh,' Yellow Hair, all those sun cycles past," said Strong Wing.

"It was on a Summer Solstice, if I recall," Red Feather added. "My grandmother, who I knew as my mother, was sakimaxkwe then. My mother died when I was born. Grandmother raised me as her own child. My mother was her only daughter, so she groomed me to become sakimaxkwe when she went to live with the Ancestors. She had seen more than seven tens of sun cycles when she died." *I have no idea why I shared that personal story with a complete stranger.* Red Feather blushed and looked away.

"The weather should be accommodating for a trip down to the beach. Perhaps you will find something worth putting in your trade packs," Bear Claw suggested.

"We always keep our eyes open," Blue Deer said.

CHAPTER 12
A DISCOVERY

The next morning Blue Deer, Redbone, Strong Wing, Hawkeye, Red Petal, and her sister, Greenbriar loaded into two canoes and headed downriver toward the Great Ocean.

They cleared the mainland and started across a pool of water that was wider than the river and went north as far as Redbone could see. East of the narrow body of water, there was a narrow band of mudflat before a low hill rose to a bit over a man's height above the calm blue water and ran parallel to it. The low hill was covered with bunchgrasses more than waist high. Many large, long-legged birds lined the shallow water along the mud bank. On the west side of the water were more mudflats with more of that tall grass and countless numbers of those wading birds. The birds varied in color—dark gray, light blue, brown, and bright white. Some had more than one color. Some had yellow legs, some had black legs. They all seemed to be hunting small fish, crabs, and various other small creatures. Swinging his view around to the south, the river bank was more irregular with woody vegetation, and the coast turned back to the west out of sight.

As they slid across the glassy water, Redbone could hear the crashing of the surf. The individual waves hitting the beach seemed to combine into a dull roar with the accent of a louder crash as a closer wave landed on the packed sand somewhere over that low ridge ahead of them.

Strong Wing led them to a shallow channel through the mud flats and into the tall grasses on the low ridge. The pounding of the surf grew louder. When they hit the end of the channel, Strong Wing stopped his canoe, and the younger people climbed out while he steadied the watercraft. Blue Deer slid his canoe to a stop on the north side of the channel so he and Redbone could step out onto the matted grass plants.

From there, they followed a trail that led to the top of the low ridge. The mud quickly became damp sand, then dry sand as they moved up the gentle slope. When he topped the ridge, Redbone noted they were in a low swale that led to another ridge about six or seven tens of paces away. Beyond that ridge lay the beach, whose surf was much louder now. Clearing the second ridge, Redbone was greeted by the wide beach. It went straight to the north as far as he could see and south a ten-tens-of-tens of paces before it turned west, out of sight. Only open salt water could be seen from there to the southern horizon.

"There is a storm coming in," Strong Wing declared.

"How can you tell?" Redbone asked. There was not a cloud to be seen in any direction. Unhindered, he could see a very long distance to the east and south.

"These waves are much bigger than they should be with this calm breeze. A storm is coming up the coast from the south. At least two days away, but you can see the slant of the waves as they come ashore.

"I see that now. Thank you for pointing that out. We were on salt water briefly when we went to Blue Crab Village and as we made our way to Lenape Town. But the air here smells saltier than there." Redbone was using all his senses to take in the magnificence of the Great Ocean. He was awed by the power of the waves as they pounded into the packed sand at the water's edge.

Hawkeye, Red Petal, and Greenbriar were running along the top fringe of water as it washed up the sand, stopped, and receded back to the ocean.

Strong Wing walked north about ten-tens of paces and stopped. Swinging his hand toward the sand at his feet, he said, "This is where Yellow Hair lay on the sand. He was an unmoving mass when the children pointed him out. Bright-Eyed Boy and Little Star were the first to notice him. My friend and I were in the surf looking for live crabs when Little Star screamed. Long Branch and I ran up here as quickly as we could to find out what was wrong. Grandfather hobbled up and started poking him with his walking stick.

"At first we were not sure what was laying here in a heap. We questioned if it was even alive. Finally, he responded to Grandfather poking him. He rolled to his hands and knees. I thought he looked more human than anything. He was completely naked so I could see he was male easy enough. But his skin was sunburned red and scratched from head to toe. None of us had ever seen hair as yellow as his.

"Finally, Grandfather prodded him into standing up. He looked younger than me but stood just as tall, even in his weakened and slumped state. I wanted to give him water. Grandfather did not want me to, but I did anyway. He was grateful. I think that moment is when we became brothers. His eyes told me how thankful he was for that little taste of water.

"We escorted him to our canoe and brought him back to the village. He was weak and exhausted when he stood in front of Grandmother. She demanded to hear where he came from. His eyes rolled, and his life soul left his body. When he collapsed at her feet, Grandmother had her healer tend to his scratched and bruised skin, but she did not allow him into the village until it was determined he would live.

"The healer covered his skin with bear grease

and powdered slippery elm bark with a little mint mixed in. They laid him by the palisade near the entrance. Grandmother told me and my brother, Clamshell, to watch him."

"That is an incredible story," said Redbone.

Redbone looked the area over carefully, but after more than two-tens of sun cycles, he knew he would find nothing. They wandered down to the high waterline and walked north along the beach looking for unusual shells or anything else that caught their eyes. Hawkeye, Red Petal, and Greenbriar were far up the beach when Hawkeye saw something in the sand. Redbone could see him bend over, then drop to his knees. Suddenly he jumped to his feet and waved his arms to get their attention.

"What have you found, Hawkeye?" Strong Wing demanded.

"Not sure, but it is unusual!" Hawkeye shouted.

Redbone, Strong Wing, and Blue Deer walked up together to see what Hawkeye had found. It was a grayed piece of wood, buried in the sand.

"You got excited over a piece of driftwood buried in the sand on a beach?" Strong Wing scoffed.

Blue Deer was bored and sorry he came on this adventure. Now they were a long way from the canoe, and all the food was back at their campsite.

Redbone looked carefully and agreed with Hawkeye that it was not just a piece of driftwood. Together they began to pull the sand away from the piece. First, they found it was much bigger that it first appeared. Then, they could see it was shaped somehow. It appeared to be on its side edge and buried deep in the sand. They continued pulling sand away from a flat surface. The object was longer than a man and at least four fingers thick.

Strong Wing began to remember, *Tor talking about riding a large piece of wood—a piece of their great canoe—across the Ocean. The waves in the surf ripped it away from him, and he never saw it again. Could this be it? I have never seen a piece of driftwood that looked like this!*

Strong Wing bent to the task of digging the big piece of wood from the beach. They worked tirelessly. As they got deeper, the color of the wood faded from gray to dark orange and finally to dark yellow, like a piece of pine that had been kept out of the sun. *It almost seems that the flat surface had been smoothed with a block of sandstone. I can see this plank was nearly an arm length wide, pointed at one end and flat at the other. Curiously, there are four rows of dark-red, round spots from one end to the other. Yellow Hair talked about pounding nails into the deck to hold it in place. I never understood what he was talking about.*

Hawkeye quietly slipped to the other side of the big board and began digging on that side.

"Look, there is something sticking out of this side. I know not what it is!" Hawkeye called to the others.

His discovery was a hard, flaky object protruding from the plank about a hand and a half.

It was dark red to orange colored, rough, and cold. When he wrapped his hand around the object, orange powder rubbed off onto his skin. It smelled and tasted strangely metallic. Then he grabbed it again and put pressure against it. The thing snapped off like a twig, leaving a sharp, jagged point on the piece in his hand and also sticking barely out of the board.

"Surely this brittle thing would not be strong enough to hold that great canoe together. No wonder it broke apart and sank," said Hawkeye.

"I do not know. It looks as if there were many of those sticking through this board. Maybe altogether, there was enough strength to hold it together until they hit those rocks. That is when it broke apart."

They went back to work digging the plank out of the sand. When they had the big plank free of its sand prison, they saw that there had been ten-and-six of those dark-red spines. Two were bent against the plank. Ten-and-two were nothing but short, sharp spikes. Four, including the one Hawkeye broke off, still protruded one and a half hands from the plank. Those four felt fragile.

They tried to lift the whole plank to see if they could haul it back to Willet Village. The thing was so heavy, they doubted it would float.

"Lying in that damp sand all this time, it has become completely waterlogged—like a log trapped in a river for many sun cycles. If we could get it to the lagoon, we would never get it to the village before it sank." Blue Deer looked at the plank, then the grass barrier on the sand dunes, shaking his head.

"I think we should put it back in the hole and bury it with sand. It should remain here as a testament to the strength and courage of Yellow Hair. Let the sand protect it for all time." Redbone spoke the words reverently while looking out across the sea.

"Well said, Redbone. Does anyone disagree?" Strong Wing took charge. He started to put the piled sand back in the hole, which had a finger of water at the bottom already.

All nodded their heads and joined in re-burying the plank that had carried Yellow Hair across the Great Ocean.

CHAPTER 13

CHANGES

Back in Willet Village, the group of explorers reported their finding and their final decision about what they had found to Red Feather and Bear Claw.

"Did it ever occur to you that you should have reported your finding to the Sakimaxkwe of Willet Village and asked for guidance before just burying such an item?" Red Feather asked.

"My apologies, Sakimaxkwe. The plank was my uncle's, and I felt the best place for it was where Hawkeye found it. I think it would rot rather quickly once exposed to the air, like a log pulled from a muddy riverbank. Once exposed to air, those water-logged limbs and trunks disappear quickly," Redbone said.

"You are right, of course. It is just that we have nothing but memories of that remarkable young man, and those are fading with each passing sun cycle," Red Feather remarked.

"But knowing an important piece of his past lies buried in the sands in our lands is a gift," Bear Claw added.

"Well said, War Chief," Blue Deer said.

"I saw it first," Greenbriar announced.

"Yes, I would have walked right by if Greenbriar had not pointed it out," said Hawkeye.

"Your head was filled with thinking about Red Petal," Greenbriar replied.

"What is this? Hawkeye, is she serious? Are you courting Red Petal? You know a relationship between you is incest, right?" Red Feather demanded.

"We are well aware we are closely related, Mother. We are cousin friends, no more. You all know we have been friends for sun cycles." Hawkeye bristled in his defense.

"Until now, she has been a child, and it was not a worry. Now that she is a woman, you must be mindful of your clan responsibilities. That includes appearances. You do understand that?" Red Feather remained rigid.

"I do wish we could discuss this in private. You are embarrassing me, Mother."

"It is far better to be embarrassed than outcast or put to death by your own clan for committing incest."

"There has never been the smallest inkling of a thought of committing incest on my part or Red

Petal's. We know who we are!" Hawkeye's fists knotted in anger.

Red Petal looked at her moccasins, her hair falling over her face in hopes of hiding her red cheeks. She tried to hide the fact that she did have incestuous feelings for Hawkeye. It was not missed by Red Feather.

"All right, everyone is dismissed except Red Petal and Hawkeye. The rest of you go about whatever you wish—it will be sunset soon and the dancing will start with all the people here already. Two days until the ceremonies begin, so go get in the mood!" Red Feather declared.

Bear Claw stayed behind until Red Feather shooed him out. "I said everyone! Now go." She pushed him in the back.

When everyone was gone, she turned to Hawkeye and Red Petal. "Now, what is this all about? Do you two have improper feelings toward one another?" Her eyes bored into both young adults.

"No, absolutely not!" said Hawkeye.

Red Petal looked at the floor and confessed in a whisper, "Yes, some I think. I cannot explain it. I just want to be with Hawkeye."

"Child, do you know what you are saying?" Red Feather asked.

Hawkeye gaped at Red Petal in disbelief. He wanted to go join the party...go anywhere except where he was. *Red Petal has more courage than I do. I believe it is time to bid her farewell until she is a happily married woman. I do not see how I can fight my parents..*

"I...I...am just so confused. But I know when I am with Hawkeye, I am happier than any other times." Tears ran down Red Petal's cheeks.

Red Feather hugged Red Petal and said, "Oh child, we will get through this. We need to find you a man who will show you what love is really about."

"That is the thing—I do not want anyone else. I feel some inner spirit pulling me to Hawkeye." She was openly crying now.

Her own demons stuck a stiletto into Red Feather's heart. In truth Bear Claw, as a young warrior, went on a raid on a Great Crab Bay village when a rakish trader came to Willet Village. Red Feather had seduced him, and it led to a pregnancy. Bear Claw was back in time for the child to be his, but she knew it had been the trader's seed that had planted in her womb. Now she was faced with two young people who may have a legitimate love for one another, and the whole village knew.

Hawkeye felt the pain in his mother's heart, causing him confusion.

"What is it, Mother? I can see the pain in your face."

For the first time, Red Petal looked up at Red Feather. She saw the pain behind the troubled woman's eyes. *What is troubling her? This is serious.*

Finally, Red Feather found her resolve.

"You two stay away from each other during this

celebration. You cannot be together. Red Petal, we will find a solution to your broken heart. Hawkeye, you have pahsahëmen games to prepare for. You are both dismissed." Red Feather's voice sounded detached from her souls.

Outside the longhouse, Red Petal turned to Hawkeye and asked, "You really just consider me a cousin friend? I thought we had much more than that. I know I love you...as a woman loves a man."

"Right now, I do not know what I feel. I know love between us is wrong, but somehow I am drawn to you. I enjoy my time with you more than any maiden I have ever met. It is so confusing. I was surprised to hear you confess your feelings for me. I think that threw me off balance. I am sorry if I hurt you."

"What you just said means more than what you said in there. I know you were afraid of your parents' reaction."

"Would you consider going away with me?"

"Where?"

"I do not know. Perhaps we could go back with Redbone to his Monongahela lands. It sounds like his family is welcoming, and they could use more warriors to fill their ranks. He plans to go west trading. I think there would be room for us in his mother's longhouse."

"I think the people will make it very uncomfortable for us in Willet Village or Sun Town. Especially my mother and the Great Sakimaxkwe. There are great stories about couples caught up in forbidden love stories. Maybe we are living one of those legends." She desperately wanted to take his hand into hers, but the time and place was just wrong.

"Perhaps. You make it sound exciting. I am worried our clansmen will track us down and kill us."

———

RED FEATHER WENT to her chamber, gut twisting. He called himself *Freebird, though I doubt that was his given name. I know he bedded at least six women in the village whose husbands were in the war party. Two others were born the same moon as Hawkeye. One in the Turkey Clan. She had a girl, and the young woman has a nose shaped like Hawkeye. Of course, Bear Claw would never notice such things.*

Bear Claw knows the truth, but how can we admit it after all these sun cycles. Yes, it would free Hawkeye to marry Red Petal, but the scandal could destroy Willet Village. Lenape Town would be happy to take advantage of our weakness and force us into the Great Crab Bay alliance.

No good can come of this situation. The simplest answer would be to send Hawkeye away someplace and get Red Petal interested in another man. She would see through that plot in a heartbeat and go find Hawkeye on her own.

What do I do? Tell Bear Claw and let him make a

decision? He has had his share of other women and encouraged me to have my fun as well. He was not even upset when I slept with Traveler just to get information about Yellow Hair and his summons to Cahokia. Bear Claw returned to this longhouse when Traveler and I were still in our sleeping chamber—not sleeping.

But I lost that baby when all of Willet Village was celebrating a new baby in the Turtle Clan lineage. It was his idea to take the newborn baby from those poor farmers just up the Mullica. He went and gave that farmer ten weights of corn seed for a baby they could not feed. He brought the baby to me while mine lay dead in my womb. We told everyone I had the baby in our sleeping chamber, then took the child to the women's lodge so the whole village would believe our story. No one ever found out what happened to the missing corn seed, and I have no idea what happened to the dead baby I delivered in my sleeping chamber. Maybe I should bring it up with him...

The door hanging pulled back, and Bear Claw entered their sleeping chamber.

"I saw Hawkeye and Red Petal walking to the Sun Town Camp. What happened? And what had you so upset?" Bear Claw asked.

"First, I told them to go their separate ways and not be seen together." A long pause. "Husband, we have a dark secret to discuss. I need your help figuring a way out of this mess."

"What mess?"

"Please listen. It will take some time. Do you

remember..." She started with him joining a war party to go on a war walk against Oyster Shell Village. She told about her tryst with a trader, and that the baby she lost may not have been his. He went and risked everything by stealing corn seed from a clan granary and traded it for a baby from a local independent farmer. What should they do about it all?

"This is a mess. The simplest solution is to keep Hawkeye and Red Petal apart. But I agree it may not be fair or just. On the other hand, they are young and can get over the loss. If we decide to admit he is not our son, and I am not crazy about that idea, the Council, or even some clan members, may not see it our way and sentence them to death anyway. They could be hunted down and killed no matter where they go."

"I have thought about that. And I thank you for keeping a cool head about this while we seek a solution. You are a better husband than I deserve."

"Ha! That was a time when fidelity did not mean a whole lot to either of us. I was so interested in becoming war chief, I neglected you and your needs. I thank you for not putting my things outside your lodge while I played war games and lifted skirts in faraway places. But if all this comes out because our son, who is not really our son, can marry his brother's daughter, there is no telling how the pieces will fall."

She leaned over and kissed him on the mouth

with more passion than he had experienced in a long time. They left the chamber a hand of time later with smiles, but no solutions to the problem with Hawkeye and Red Petal.

———

RED PETAL and Hawkeye managed to get Redbone away from the others in Sun Town. They had a plan to discuss.

"Redbone, when do you plan to go back to New Long Pine Village?" Hawkeye asked.

"That will be up to Blue Deer. I am traveling in his canoe, and we plan to trade along the way. Why do you ask?"

"It is complicated, but Red Petal and I have fallen in love. But, according to our customs, we are too closely related. But we feel strongly that something is not right. It is just a feeling. My brother is married to Red Petal's mother. Red Petal feels that the connection between Strong Wing and me is not strong enough for us to be true brothers."

"Yes. I can feel the bond between myself and my sister, Greenbriar. But that bond is not there with Strong Wing and Hawkeye. True, there are more sun cycles between them, but brothers should have something stronger that ties them together. Does that make sense?" Red Petal asked.

"I see what you are saying. My sister is two sun cycles younger than me, and I feel many of her emotions. You may have noticed that I feel a strong connection to my aunt and her husband, and they left our village before I was born. I have never met them, yet I feel something whenever I even think about them. And finding that plank today. It was like I could feel Yellow Hair right there with us. His souls became part of that board and still reside in it."

"Does Blue Deer plan to take you all the way back to your home, then come back here alone?" Red Petal asked Redbone.

"As far as I know."

"What if there was another way?" Hawkeye asked.

"Such as?"

"What if, after the Solstice Celebration winds down, Red Petal and I load your things in a canoe, and the three of us go to your home?" she asked.

"Would we have ten warriors after us to bring you back? I do not think I wish to be mixed up in anything that will cause trouble and hard feelings. I am a trader and must live by the code of traders that keeps the power of trade strong and honest. I would not wish to be accused of kidnapping people from high-ranking clans," Redbone replied.

"If I can arrange the blessings of our clans?"

"That would make all the difference for me."

"I have my own canoe," Hawkeye said.

"And I think I can get us away from our clans," Red Petal added.

OVER THE NEXT THREE DAYS, Hawkeye and Red Petal kept their proper distance. Both played on their respective pahsahëmen teams, and the final game of the competition featured the men from Willet Village against the women from Sun Town. This time, the Sun Town women bested the Willet Village men.

The dancing lasted until the sky lightened the next morning. With little sleep, the various villages packed up their camps and prepared to paddle their way up the Mullica River, portage and float to the Lenape River, and disperse up the Lenape to their respective villages.

Strong Wing and Willow Branch would spend another day at the request of Sakimaxkwe Red Feather. When all the others had left, Red Feather invited Willow Branch, Strong Wing, and Red Petal, along with Redbone and Blue Deer, to join her, Bear Claw, and Hawkeye for tea under a thatch-roofed pavilion. All other people were kept out of hearing range by Turkey Clan warriors.

"I know we are all very tired from the recent activities and long nights. However, something of great importance concerning all of us has arisen, and we need to develop a solution that is amenable to each of us."

Everyone sipped their tea and awaited further explanation from Red Feather.

"It seems that two of our young people have

fallen in love. Normally this is a time of joy and cele-bration. This time, there are complications that must be addressed. The couple involved are my son, Hawkeye, and Willow Branch's daughter, Red Petal. These two grew up as cousins and have always been very close despite the fact they live ten days apart. But now, with both passed into adulthood, the situa-tion has become a problem."

"Of course, we cannot allow such close relatives to become husband and wife," Willow Branch added.

"This situation is more complicated, I am afraid. And it is all our fault." Red Feather looked to Bear Claw for support and got a nod. "Ten-and-eight sun cycles past, my husband was striving to earn the respect and support of the Willet Village warrior society and went, as deputy war chief, on a war walk to Oyster Shell Village on Great Crab Bay. During his absence, I was guilty of an indiscretion with a visiting trader. Shortly after the trader left the village, Bear Claw returned. I was pregnant, but I said the child was Bear Claw's and everyone believed that was true."

Hawkeye looked at Bear Claw and Red Feather with a million questions in his eyes.

She continued, "The truth is that the trader was the father. Then, late in the pregnancy, I lost the baby. But Bear Claw, being the great man that he is, never questioned the timing of the pregnancy, slipped off to a local farmer he knew just had a baby, traded stolen seed corn for that child, and brought the him back so that everyone in Willet Village would think I gave birth to a healthy baby. So, in truth, Strong Wing and Hawkeye are not related, although everyone in Willet Village believes they are full brothers. If the truth comes out now, the Council of Elders will probably select a new sakimaxkwe and war chief. We could be shamed, even outcast. Our supporters could revolt."

"Our warriors often go on raids to steal children and slaves. What was the problem?" Strong Wing asked.

"The difference was that I snuck away and traded a child for stolen corn seed without sanction of the War Council or the Council of Elders. You should know that such actions are outlawed and result in severe penalties." Bear Claw's face had lost all color. His eyes betrayed near panic.

"It is not my place to address this serious matter for your family and clan, but I have a solution I think would work, at least temporarily," said Redbone.

Everyone looked at him like they thought he was crazy, but Redbone held his head high.

"Red Petal and Hawkeye could accompany me to New Long Pine Village. You have shown that Hawkeye and Strong Wing are not technically related, so no gods would be offended. They could marry by Monongahela customs, which are not so different from yours. They can establish their marriage in my village, and, after a few sun cycles, return to Sun Town or Willet Village as a normal couple and no fuss would be made."

Everyone looked at Redbone with a variety of expressions.

Red Feather said, "That just might work."

"I agree with the temporary part. My daughter should live and raise her children in Sun Town. However, I can see where this could solve the immediate issues. Strong Wing?"

"We will need to convince the Councils and the people these two did not run off to get married. Surely we can do that," Strong Wing replied.

"I think we can make it work for Willet Village," Red Feather added.

"Wait. Do our laws not say that adopted family members are the same as natural ones, and follow the same rules on incest?" Strong Wing asked.

"Yes, but this where it becomes messy. You see, Hawkeye was raised as our natural child. No adoption was made. The fact that we did not adopt him is probably a bigger scandal than Hawkeye and Red Petal getting married." Red Feather looked at Hawkeye to gauge his reaction.

"Then my whole life is a lie! Now I really want to go with Redbone and Red Petal to any place but here!" Hawkeye burst out.

"You are still my son in my heart," Red Feather said quietly.

"You are as dead to me as the baby you threw

away!" Hawkeye got up and walked away. Red Petal chased after him.

Redbone, Red Petal, Hawkeye, and Blue Deer rested the next whole day to prepare for the arduous trip back to New Long Pine Village. Blue Deer would accompany them to the mouth of the Juniata River.

Redbone's packs were heavy with conch and other east coast shells, Willet Village pottery, tobacco twists, Lenape-style clay pipes, shell gorgets and beads, a few deer, fox, raccoon, bobcat, mountain lion, and bear pelts.

CHAPTER 14

FRIENDS

After tearful goodbyes, two canoes set out up Mullica River. Red Feather and Bear Claw were nowhere near the canoe landing. After three days paddling and a short portage, they arrived in Lenape Town. The village was still recovering from its own Solstice Celebration. Some campsites were still occupied north of the large village. The faces they encountered betrayed fatigue and too little sleep.

Blue Deer advised Redbone's party to wait at their canoes while he went into the village, which was not surrounded by a palisade. He needed to tell some war leader of their purpose, inform Tanager of his situation, and secure some more provisions for their continued journey. In just over two fingers of time, he returned with two bags heavily laden with nuts, corn cakes, and jerky. It was midafternoon when they took to the river. They would arrive in

Blue Crab Village in time for evening meal and find place to sleep.

In Blue Crab Village, Blue Deer found a very happy Water Racer. His new life as a hunter in his wife's clan was obviously successful. He invited the whole party to join him for evening meal in the Turtle Clan longhouse, where they would be welcome to sleeping pallets as well.

Water Racer was especially proud that his wife was with child, though she still did not show. She seemed happy as well, which pleased Blue Deer and Redbone.

"You did not find a maiden of your own at the Solstice Celebration in Willet Village?" Water Racer asked Redbone.

"I had little time for such things there. But we did go down to the beach where they had found Yellow Hair, and after all this time, Hawkeye here found the very board that carried Yellow Hair across the Great Ocean. It was a religious experience for me," Redbone replied. His eyes drifted somewhere, unfocused, as he spoke.

"You have a real attachment to him. I have never seen anything like it," Water Racer said as he slapped Redbone on the back and led them to the main firepit where they would join the Turtle Clan for evening meal.

Blue Deer handled the formal introductions, leaving out all the controversial details of the presence of Red Petal and Hawkeye. The elders around the firepit were most interested in Redbone's story. They were impressed with his mobility despite his clubfoot.

"I was born with it and never considered it a problem. But I recognize that I cannot move quickly and am not suitable on a war walk. I guess that is why I chose to become a trader," he explained.

The elders and Spring Flower's family noted how well Redbone commanded the Lenape tongue. Overall, the group was well received by the Turtle Clan, but they were cool toward Hawkeye and Red Petal, as they considered the River Lenape enemies even though they were invited guests for that night.

The next morning, after a small meal, they were on the Mud River working their way north against the strong current. Hawkeye and Redbone soon learned to work together to propel their craft efficiently upriver. Blue Deer convinced Water Racer to accompany him for the day and one-half trip to the Juniata River where Redbone and his party would depart for the west on an increasingly used trade route.

Of course, they were compelled to spend a night in Ottertail Village and have a short trade session in the morning before heading upriver to the Juniata. They went ashore at the Juniata where Blue Deer and Redbone spent a finger of time in an emotional goodbye.

"Now the work begins, my friends. The Juniata is a gentle river near the mouth, but soon enough the hills make it a fast-moving, rocky, and challenging river. There will be many portages, and we are carrying a lot of weight. Red Petal, are you sure you are up to the strenuous journey we are about to undertake?"

"I will do my share. I can work as hard as any woman and most men." Red Petal raised her chin and spoke with confidence.

"All right, let us get started!" Redbone announced.

The rest of the morning they followed the meanders of the lower Juniata. As they neared the place where Yellow Hair led the successful fight against Haudenosaunee raiders, Redbone explained the battle, then pointed out the place it took place. When they reached the site where Yellow Hair had set up his decoy campsite, Redbone directed them to the shore, and they ate some corncakes and venison jerky. Redbone lit a small fire so Red Petal could make them a bag of sassafras tea.

The day was hot and humidity high. Redbone and Hawkey were dressed in breechclouts and low moccasins. Each had a rabbit skin on their head to provide a little shade. Red Petal had on a doeskin loincloth, low moccasins, and a floppy woven grass hat. All were sweating profusely and drinking frequently from water skins.

While they were stopped, Red Petal suggested they swim to wash the sweat from their bodies and cool off. Hawkeye enthusiastically joined her as they swam across the river. Redbone hung back and stayed in the shallows. He was not confident in his ability to swim any distance with his bad foot.

When Red Petal and Hawkeye reached the small cove on the far side, they discovered Redbone was not with them. Looking back, Red Petal saw Redbone splashing in the shallows near their picnic site.

She turned to Hawkeye and embraced him. His physical response was immediate. She kissed him deeply in waist-deep water as their emotions heated. With no little sister or mother around to diminish her passion, she took advantage of the situation. She had her loincloth and his breechclout off before they were out of the water. They found a place with thick, tall grasses and no rocks.

After several heartbeats of standing, kissing, and exploring each other's bodies, they laid down in the soft green grass and coupled for the first time. She found herself in a dreamworld of pleasure despite the small jab of pain when he first entered her. She had often fantasized about how it would feel, but actually feeling his manhood in her woman hole far exceeded her expectations.

"You fill me," she hoarsely whispered in his ear.

"And you surround me with your warmth." His voice was cut short as his passion exploded into her, leaving him breathless.

She was just behind him as her pleasure contractions expelled his softening manhood.

They panted together, sweat-drenched bodies pushed hard against each other.

"Next time, wait for me, please," she begged.

"I promise. Your heat and strength took me by surprise. And I have been waiting for this for so long, it was just overwhelming."

"I understand, my love."

Almost involuntarily, her thigh pushed against his soft, wet manhood. She wanted more. He responded and soon they were locked in the coital position again. This time he was able to control his climax until after she reached her pinnacle of pleasure.

"That was everything I could ask for, my lover," she moaned.

"Yes-s-s," he whispered breathlessly. "Redbone must think we drowned. We should get back, I suppose."

"As much as I would like to stay in this place with you all day, I guess you are right."

"I hope we did not make a baby," he said.

"Why?"

"I do not want this hindered by a growing belly for a long time. Besides, I think we need to get settled and married first."

"You are right, of course. I was worried you found some fault with me," she said as she stood up.

A visible wet spot was on the matted grass where she had been. And in the middle of the wet place was a small splotch of blood. A glob of thick, pink moisture slid down her inner thigh. *That will be washed off by the time we reach the other side,* she hoped.

She slipped her damp loincloth on and he his still-wet breechclout. Holding hands, they walked back into the water and started the swim to the other side.

"I was beginning to think you ran off on me! Thought maybe you had second thoughts about going over the mountains." Redbone smiled and winked, assuring them he knew what they were up to. *I wish a beauty like her would take a liking to me. The only coupling I have ever known is in my dreams and using my own hand.*

"Are you well, Redbone? Your face had a strange look for a minute, like your stomach was unsettled with something," Red Petal asked in a caring voice.

"It is nothing," Redbone stoically replied.

She shrugged her shoulders and climbed into her place among the packs in the middle of the canoe. Hawkeye was ready to push them into the river and jump in as soon as Redbone was settled in the front of the craft. They paddled all afternoon and into the evening without rest. Finally, they reached a used campsite Blue Deer had pointed out to Redbone.

"Make for that small canoe landing, and we will make camp here. Tomorrow we will have our first portage, and the current will get stronger. We will also pass a small village. We can decide then if we wish to stop. With your strong paddling, we are making good time so far," Redbone announced.

When the canoe slid to a stop, Redbone caught a movement at the back of the camp. Careful inspection showed it was a fat groundhog near a fresh mound of dirt. He signaled for the others to sit still. He stealthily pulled his bow and quiver from just behind him, awkwardly strung the bow and pulled an arrow. Neither Hawkeye nor Red Petal could see what his target was and thought the worst.

Finally, Redbone had his bow up and drawn back. He let the arrow fly, waited for the arrow to hit, and announced, "Fresh meat tonight!"

"What is it? I could not see anything," Hawkeye asked.

"Just a large, fat groundhog. We have a good meal or two, and I can add a mediocre summer hide to my collection."

"I am starved! I will get a fire going," Red Petal declared.

"I will gather firewood," Hawkeye added.

In no time, they had a comfortable camp set up with bed rolls laid out, a hot fire going in an old fire ring, the groundhog roasting on a spit, and a tea bag warming on a tripod close to the fire.

The trio sat around the fire waiting for the meat to cook. Hawkeye lowered his head and sniffed his armpit.

"I believe I will go for another swim after evening meal!" Hawkeye declared.

"I will join you," Red Petal chimed in.

"I will wash upriver far enough away so you two can have your privacy," Redbone added.

After they ate, Redbone went upstream around a bend to do his cleansing. Red Petal suggested Hawkeye take her on her bedroll before they went into the river to swim and clean their bodies. When they went into the water, the first thing they noticed was the water was much cooler than it had been downriver. Still, it did not take them long to acclimate. They were sitting in water that barely floated her well-formed breasts.

"I think Redbone is terribly lonely," she said seriously to Hawkeye.

"He has chosen the trader life. He knows it is a life of solitude. No woman wants a husband who is a trader. He will never be home for any length of time. That is not a life for a woman. You have me, why do you care about him?"

"He is a friend and a loyal one. Do you not want him to be happy?"

"Of course, I do. But happy to him is plying a river, making a good trade, and seeing new things. Did you see his face when we dug up that old plank in the sand?"

"Yes. That plank belonged to the Yellow Hair he is always talking about. If I heard right that man was gone before Redbone was even born. I do not see how he could be so attached to someone he never met."

"Yellow Hair was married to Redbone's aunt. It is

like a cherished family member you never had a chance to meet. They become greater, like a myth or a legend. I think Yellow Hair is bigger in Redbone's mind like that. Probably if he ever met him, he would be disappointed."

They heard footfalls coming around the corner. The sun had set, but it was not dark yet. Red Petal and Hawkeye stood and walked out of the water. The air had cooled with the sunset, and her nipples stood at attention.

Redbone tried not to ogle as he walked up but found it impossible to take his eyes from her perfect breasts. Hawkeye noticed Redbone's eyes glued to Red Petal's fabulous body. Swallowing his pride, thinking of what she said earlier and noticing Redbone's manhood bulging against his breechclout in the dim light, he made a strange suggestion.

"I think I would like to take a walk alone. Red Petal, how about you and Redbone stay here and get to know one another? I promise I will not be jealous, and I think Redbone needs to relieve some tension. Are you amenable?"

She looked toward Hawkeye, but it was too dark to read his eyes. *I am the one to suggest Redbone needs a woman, and I am the only one here. I guess I could do it this once, since Hawkeye suggested it.*

"Is that something you desire, Redbone?" she asked. Then she noticed Hawkeye was already walking away.

As soon as Hawkeye was out of sight, Red Petal took Redbone's hand and pulled him to her.

"I...I...have...never..."

She cut him off with a wet kiss on his lips. He melted into her. Her firm breasts with those hardened nipples pressed into his bare chest. Her warm hands slipped up to his face and pulled his mouth hard against hers. Her tongue pushed into his mouth and explored. He reciprocated. One of her hands dropped to the thong holding her loincloth over her shapely hips.

His erection was painfully restrained in his breechclout. She slid her hand across his breechclout, squeezing his confined manhood. She deftly untied the thong holding his breechclout up and brushed it off his erection until it fell to the ground. He tentatively slid his hand over her firm breast and pressed his palm into her hard nipple. She moaned.

She slid her hand down and cupped his scrotum and fondled his testicles. He gasped into her mouth. He squeezed her breast, and she moaned into his mouth. She slid her hand up and loosely gripped his manhood. Again, he gasped into her mouth. She slid her hand the length of his penis, got to the end and felt his wetness. She gripped a little harder and started to slide her hand back toward the base of his manhood. He moaned aloud into her mouth, and his seed exploded across her belly and over her hand.

She jerked her hand away when she felt his hot

seed splash on her. She pulled her mouth away from his.

"Oh, I did not expect that!" she exclaimed.

"I am so sorry," he nearly cried. "I never felt such sensations. My body…"

"Shh. It is not over. You will revive in a few heartbeats and take me properly. I am going down to the landing and wash this off me, and we will start again."

"You…you do…not need to…do that. I…will be all right."

"No. We need to know each other properly. Stopping now will only leave a bad feeling in your heart. You need to know the full joy of love."

"But you love Hawkeye. Should you not give all your love to him?"

"If it were not for you, Hawkeye and Red Petal would be lost in a tangle of clan laws and rules. You deserve my love and gratitude. Come over to the river with me, and I will wash you up too."

After she washed herself and Redbone's genitals, he was already responding to her touch. With her body pressed against his, he moved a hand down and gripped her tight buttocks. She responded with a low moan into his mouth. She took his hand and led him to her bedroll.

Carefully, she dropped to her knees and pulled him down to her. She kissed him deeply as she was dropping onto her back. She pulled him on top of her. Next, she pulled her tongue from his mouth and softly said, "Get to know me with your fingers." She pulled his hand to her patch of damp, black pubic hair.

He did as she requested. When he found her folds, he learned they were warm, wet, and inviting. He slid a finger into her woman hole, and she moaned into his ear. He explored deeper, eliciting more moans, then she squeezed his finger with her woman muscles. He felt his erect penis grow even harder.

Again, she slid her hand along his manhood. This time, she nearly begged, "Take me, Redbone. I want you in me. Please, take me!"

He worked to his knees, trying to position himself to enter her. She took over and guided his erection into her with her hand. Next, she moved both hands to his hard buttocks and pulled him into her.

"Yesss!" she moaned.

He felt his whole penis as she swallowed it with her woman hole. When he thought he could go no deeper, she rocked her hips into him, and he plunged deeper. She squeezed the length of him as she wrapped her legs around his thighs and pulled tighter.

She relaxed and pulled back slightly, then pulled and squeezed again. He quickly got the rhythm, and they were soon in a rocking tangle of coital pleasure.

Her moans grew louder and more frantic as he began to groan like a giant oak tree in a windstorm.

Finally, every muscle in her body contacted, and she screamed her pleasure as she pulled every drop of his seed into her body. They were so wound up. They could not just relax when it was over. After contractions shook both their bodies for several heartbeats as their bodied slowed and heart rates lowered.

"That was incredible, Red Petal. I will never forget this." The words were interrupted with panting and kissing as he spoke.

"Nor will I. I thought Hawkeye would be the only one who could do that to me. I truly love him, but now I know I truly love you, too. Can a woman really, I mean REALLY, love two men?"

"I think you are living proof. But I would never want to come between you two. You have risked so much to make your love story come true. I would not want to ruin that."

"Are you saying you no longer want me?"

"Never. I want you to be happy. And we have many days of traveling together ahead of us. I do not wish to spoil it."

"Are you two finished yet?" came out of the darkness from upriver.

"Yes, you can come into camp now," Red Petal answered. She gave Redbone a quick kiss on the lips and pushed him aside as she got up and went to the river for another washing of her privates. Now she learned she was sore down there.

"I guess you did all right. I heard her cries of passion far up the river." Hawkeye's voice sounded strained, his hand on the back of his neck.

"I hope you were truly all right with this. It was far more than I expected. But I do not want to have any hard feelings with you. We have a long way to go, and we need to remain friends."

"I see no problems. I love her, she loves me. If she loves you, too, which I think she does, we will just have to work out some sort of arrangement to make it work. I will say this, though. I am willing to share her with you and no one else. But if she is not willing to share me, or you, with other women we may meet in the future, that may be a problem. What is good for one must be good for all. Agreed?"

"Yes, I see your point."

Just then, Red Petal came back from the river. She sat down on her bedroll and took Hawkeye's hand.

He pulled her hand up and kissed it before saying. "You smell clean."

"I hope so. I had to sit in that cool river while you men talked it out."

"What is there to talk out? Obviously, you love both of us, and we both love you. We are all friends and must live together very closely until we get to Redbone's home, at least. Now, what took you so long at the river?"

"Honestly, I was kind of sore down there from all the activity today, and that cool water felt good."

Redbone could not believe how open and frank both she and Hawkeye were about such private matters. *Of course, I have never been around many girls outside my own family. Maybe all are like this.*

CHAPTER 15

TROUBLE

Redbone woke up to the grunts and coos of Hawkeye and Red Petal making love less than an arm's length away from him. That was a little unsettling. He quickly noted that the sky was changing from night to the first light of day. He noted that there were a few stars still visible in the eastern sky, but the west was all black. *Must be a storm out that way.*

When he was finished studying the sky, he noted the love-making session was over. Redbone rolled out of his bedroll and tended to getting the fire going. The morning was cooler than the night had been, and the heat felt good. With the fire going, he wandered off to take care of his personal needs.

When he returned to the fire, Red Petal came back from the river. Hawkeye was nowhere to be seen in the early morning light.

"Where did Hawkeye go?" Redbone asked.

"He said it was your turn and went upriver."

"I think we should get on the river. A storm is coming, and we should get to a better camp than this one. At the end of a portage ahead, there is a good campsite with decent shelter. We may need to forgo stopping at that small settlement."

Redbone noted a sad look on her face and asked, "Are you well?" While waiting for her answer, he began heating some water in a cooking bag. "Groundhog stew." He smiled.

"Not really well, Redbone. Twice in the night, Hawkeye took me. And then again this morning. He did not even ask me. He just took me. He just whispered he did not want to wake you. He moved in me until he was finished and rolled back to his bedroll. Three times that happened. After you were away this morning, he said, 'I am going upriver. It is his turn.' He pointed at your bedroll and walked away without saying another word. I am worried about him."

"I am worried about you. He should not treat you like that. If I stay away from you, maybe he will be back to himself."

"I do not want you to stay away. I am so confused. Last night he said everything is good between all of us. Now, he is acting differently. I do not understand."

"Nor do I. Can you put the stew together, and I will go find him. We need to go as soon as we can."

"Of course. Be careful. Kiss me before you go." A tear trickled down her cheek as she stepped up to him. They embraced with a passionate kiss, and he turned and hobbled upriver.

He had put a buckskin shirt on and was now wondering if he should have put leggings on, too. He rounded the bend in the river and saw Hawkeye sitting on a rock about two hundred paces up the river. When he got within twenty paces, Hawkeye called out, "Finished already? I thought you were more of a man than that!"

"Hawkeye, I am not looking for trouble. You suggested Red Petal and I know one another. Last night you said it was all good and did not mind sharing her with me. Now you are acting strange."

"Did she tell you that? Because you and I have not spoken today. So, how do you know I am acting strange?"

"It was strange that you left without speaking to me. It was strange what you said to me when I walked up. The truth is, there is a storm coming, and we need to get a good distance upriver before it hits."

"I do not know about any storms upriver, but I know a storm is brewing between you and me. Are you going to quit Red Petal or not?"

"I told her I would if it makes you happy again. She said she did not want that. I said I would if it brings peace between us."

"You said that?"

"I told you that last night."

"And if she wants you, will you tell her no?"

"She is a hard person to say 'no' to, but I promise

you I will try. But I will say this. If you take her again without asking her, if you take her just to release your seed, you and I will have trouble."

"If she told you that behind my back, we already have trouble. She is a wife to me. The first I have ever had. I will not tolerate her talking behind my back."

"Then you better be honest with her and give her all your love."

"I will also not tolerate you telling me how I should behave. Especially with my wife."

"I do not understand you, but we need to get back to camp. Now!" Redbone turned and hobbled down the riverbank toward their camp.

When Redbone came around the bend, Red Petal jumped up and ran to him. She clutched him in her arms and kissed his cheek.

"Did you find him?"

"Yes. We had an argument. He is acting strange. I told him I would quit you to keep the peace between him and me. He was not satisfied, and we argued. I told him if he used you just to release his seed, we would have trouble. He said if you have confided in me behind his back, he and I would have trouble. He said he considered you his wife, and he will treat you as he pleases. Now I am worried about your safety."

"Me too. I feel safe around you. But can he hurt you? I mean, can you fight him with your bad foot?"

"Depends. I know I am stronger, but my foot definitely slows me down. We need to stop this and get on the river."

She still had her arm around his back. Hawkeye came around the bend. Redbone's back was toward Hawkeye. The man saw her with her arm around Redbone's back and his hand on her shoulder.

Hawkeye charged at Redbone who heard the steps in the gravel. Redbone spun around and pushed Red Petal away in the same motion. She fell in the gravel as Hawkeye plowed into Redbone. Redbone twisted with the impact and staggered while Hawkeye was knocked off his line of travel and stumbled into some bigger rocks.

Redbone recovered and stepped toward Hawkeye, who was unmoving, but he had an arm that was obviously broken.

When Redbone got to Hawkeye, Red Petal was looking at her wounded boyfriend. "What did you do?" she questioned Redbone.

"I do not know. He smashed into me and knocked me off balance. I turned, and you were just getting up, and he was like he this."

Redbone bent down to assess Hawkeye's injuries. "It appears that when Hawkeye slammed into me, he deflected off, and his momentum carried him into the rocks. Going down, he threw his arm out to break his fall, but his arm broke, then his head hit on a rock and knocked him unconscious. Can you help me get him out of these rocks and onto his bedroll? Then we can set his arm and bind it with some wood and cord. It will be better if we do that while he is unconscious."

"Yes."

Redbone took Hawkeye around his chest from behind and pulled him back. "Steady his head. Keep it from flopping around."

Together, they shuffled Hawkeye to his bedroll. Once there, Redbone checked his breathing and heartbeat. Both were detectable but weak. There was a big knot on his forehead. Then he went to Hawkeye's arm. The big bone was broken above the elbow of his left arm. From the firewood pile, Redbone picked out two straight pieces a little shorter than Hawkeye's upper arm and one that would reach from his elbow to the tips of his fingers. Then from one of his packs he pulled out a long piece of cord and some rabbit skins.

"Here is what we will do. See how the bone at the break is offset? I am going to pull the arm straight down until the broken bone slides back into place. As soon as it slides into place, wrap it with this rabbit skin, hair side against his skin. Then put the wood on both sides, the thinner one to the inside, and use the cord to wind around the two sticks until they hold the bone steady and straight. Use a good knot to hold the cord tight around the arm. Then wrap the other rabbit skin around his forearm and all the way to his fingertips. Put the long stick under his arm, Wrap and tie the cord from his elbow to his fingers, being careful not to cut off the circulation to his fingers. Then we can put the arm in a sling. It should heal by the time we reach my homelands. Are you ready?"

"Yes, let us get this over."

The procedure went as Redbone instructed. Hawkeye moaned while Redbone was setting the bone, but did not awaken. While Redbone was rigging Hawkeye in a sling, he had Red Petal make some slippery elm and willow bark tea and a paste to make a poultice to put on the knot on Hawkeye's forehead. He told her to sprinkle some ground mint in the tea to make it less bitter.

Redbone was just finishing the sling when Hawkeye's eyes flickered. Red Petal used a cool wet piece of deer skin tanned without the hair on it to wipe Hawkeye's cheeks and his eyelids. Hawkeye flickered his eyes again and began to moan.

"Come back to us, Hawkeye, we need you," she coaxed while watching him closely.

Hawkeye opened his eyes and struggled to focus on Red Petal. "W...what...what ha...happen? W... where am I?" he mumbled.

"We are in camp on the Juniata River. You fell down. You broke your arm and cracked your head on a rock. We set your arm and have a poultice on your head."

"W...who is w...we?"

"Redbone and me."

"Are you his woman now?"

"I am your woman."

"You lie. I saw you."

"Hawkeye, I love you both. I have room in my heart for both of you. Please do not make me choose.

I want both of you in my life. And in my bed, if you must know."

"I will not have it. You are my wife. You must do as I say."

"But we are not married yet. We must get to Redbone's land so we can be married in peace."

"No. We will go back to Willet Village and forbid Redbone from ever returning."

"No, we cannot go back to Willet Village. If we show up there, the questions and answers will destroy your parents, and maybe mine, in the bargain."

"They are not my parents. Did you not hear? That beast of a war chief stole me from my mother. I want to destroy him."

"Where is Redbone?"

"Right over here, Hawkeye. I am building a shelter that will keep us dry when the storm rolls in. We have no choice but to shelter here, so I am making it secure."

"Where is this storm? I do not trust you. You are going to make it so you and my wife can get away from me. I see that now."

"Hawkeye, your souls have been loose. They just recently came back to your body. Drink more tea so you can heal."

"You want to poison me? Why do you not just club me with a rock?"

"No one wants to harm you, Hawkeye. We love

you and want you healthy again," Red Petal pleaded while she looked at Redbone for support.

"The shelter is ready now. Let us get you into it and settled in. We can finish the groundhog stew for evening meal and be ready when the storm arrives. It must be raining hard in the west because the river is already starting to get muddy."

Redbone and Red Petal got on either side of Hawkeye and bent down to lift him to his feet. He was not a big, powerful man, and they managed to get him to his feet and held him tight. He started to swoon, but they steadied him. After a time, they coaxed him into the shelter Redbone had built from poles he scavenged and several animal hides he had in his packs.

Hawkeye's bedding was a selection of deer and elk hides and a backrest made from chunks of wood covered with a mountain lion hide. Seeing the arrangement, her bedroll next to Hawkeye's and Redbone's ten hands to the side, Red Petal moved her bedroll over to Redbone's. He looked at her with questioning eyes and she mouthed, "Trust me." They settled Hawkeye down in his bedding in a sitting position with his back against the backrest.

Seeing Red Petal's bedroll by Redbone's, Hawkeye demanded, "Woman, put your bedroll over here by your husband."

"Red Petal divorced Hawkeye for acting rude to the man who saved his life, among other things."

"What other things?"

"Treating me like a piece of property and just acting like a filthy, worm-eating snake. Your love for me was nothing but an act!"

Redbone brought the rest of the items into the shelter, including a good supply of firewood. His fire ring was built so the smoke would drift outside the tentlike structure. He rolled Hawkeye's old bedroll and placed it at the foot of his bedding.

Rain started to patter on the shelter's walls. Shortly, heavy rain was beating against their temporary home.

"Do you intend to fornicate with that woman in my presence?" Hawkeye asked Redbone.

"I will not even dignify that question with an answer."

"See if you can get some more tea down him while I get the stew warmed up, please," said Redbone to Red Petal.

"I will take nothing from that woman," Hawkeye declared.

"All right. Would you please heat up the stew, Red Petal? I will try to get the patient to take his medicine."

She laughed and set the stew bag close to the fire. Then she put the flat rock Redbone had brought in and set it on a corner of the fire ring. When it was hot enough, she would place some corncakes on the stone to heat them.

The rain thrumming on the wall coverings, exhaustion from setting up the water-proof shelter, and all the troubles with Hawkeye had Redbone ready for sleep when darkness filled their lodge. He stripped, lay down, and pulled his elk hide blanket up to his shoulders expecting Red Petal to settle a couple hands away in an effort to keep peace with Hawkeye. But she slid beneath her blanket and under his. She snugged her naked, warm body against his and draped an arm across his chest.

"Hold me, Redbone," she pleaded.

He slipped his arm around her shoulder and pulled her close. Though they were both naked, her warm body conforming to his was the last thing he remembered as sleep overcame him.

It was still dark in the shelter when he heard morning bird songs in the nearby trees and bushes. *Already? I just closed my eyes!* Then an overwhelming stench filled his nose. Red Petal was just reacting to the smell when he tried to pull his arm from around her shoulders. The appendage felt dead. He had no feeling.

She sat up, letting the blanket fall to her lap.

"What is that smell?" she cried out.

"Smells like our patient could not hold his bowels," Redbone answered. He worked himself to a sitting position and fumbled with his numb arm. He noted the walls were now a light gray color and he could see a few things in the shelter—most noticeably—her perky breasts, nipples hardened in the cool air.

At last, he was able to stand. His privates at her eye level got her full attention.

"What are we going to do with him? And what is wrong with your arm?"

"My arm fell asleep from being around you all night. I do not know what we need to do with him."

With minimum feeling in his hand and arm, he was able to get his breechclout pulled on and tied, then get his moccasins on. With the peep show over, she managed to get herself dressed in her loincloth, a shirt, leggings, and moccasins.

Redbone went to check on Hawkeye, who had yet to make a sound. Working his way between Red Petal and Hawkeye, he finally made it to Hawkeye's head. His eyes were open and sightless. Redbone bent close and listened for breathing. There was none. He touched one of eyes. No reaction.

"He is dead!" Redbone exclaimed.

"What? No, he cannot be. He is one of us!" Tears welled in her eyes, she dropped back to the bedding, laid down and began sobbing into the blankets.

"I am going to drag him out and to the river to wash him. Then we can prepare him for burial. Or should we take him to a village?"

"No. We should bury him here. Taking him to his home will lead to questions that cannot be answered. You and I must stay together—always," she declared.

Redbone bent to the task of dragging Hawkeye's body from the shelter. He just wrapped a sleeping skin around the body and pulled him out the door flap by his feet.

The area where their bedrolls had laid the day before was now a knee-deep pool of semi-clear water. It made a good place to wash Hawkeye's lifeless body. When Redbone unrolled the blanket, the extent of the man's loose bowels became very evident. More liquid than solid, and there was some blood mixed in the refuse.

Redbone respectfully removed the sling, then unwrapped the splints tied to the broken arm. There was no need to bury him with a bound arm. He carefully removed the deceased's shirt and set it aside. Then he pulled off the moccasins. Finally, he dragged the stiff body into the knee-deep water. Though it was chilly, it was not unbearable. Using a piece of the rabbit skin arm wrap, Redbone thoroughly washed the lower body, even between the stiff legs.

Red Petal stood watching as Redbone worked to get all of the foul mess from his former friend's body. When Redbone was finished from the waist down, he dragged the body to a cleaner part of the pool. She picked up another of the arm wraps, stepped into the water and began washing the upper torso. She lifted his hair and began washing the back of his neck when she saw something strange.

"Look, Redbone. What is this?"

Redbone looked at the discolored area just at the hairline at the back of the neck. As she washed the darkened area, two black dots appeared.

"Something bit him," Redbone observed, touching the spots. "This was a big spider, I think. No wonder he was acting strange. It must have been excruciating. Why did he not say something? He knew I have healing plants in my packs—we might have saved him."

Red Petal was openly crying and shaking her head. Redbone stood and held her. His strength gave her strength.

"Do you think he knew he was dying? Is that why he acted as he did?"

"Only he could answer that. Let us finish and get his body up where it will dry. I have some ochre in my pack we can use to prepare him to meet the ancestors."

"How did you know we paint symbols on our deceased before burial?" she asked.

"We have the same custom. We are more alike than we know, I think. Shall we fix some tea and corncakes while his body is drying?"

"Yes. This may sound strange, but after we bury him, I want you to make love to me."

"I can do that, if you like."

"Yes." She resumed her sobbing.

After they ate in silence, Redbone dug out a stick of red ochre, a small pot of fish oil, and an empty small ceramic pot. He placed the empty pot on the flat stone that was used for heating the corn cakes. Then, he poured a small amount of fish oil and a small piece of the red ochre into the pot. As the fish oil heated, the ochre dissolved into it. He soon had a sufficient amount of the red liquid for their purposes.

"I will let you paint the correct symbols on his body while I start preparing a suitable grave. What do you think of that prominent knoll overlooking the river?"

"Perfect."

She went to work using a finger dipped in the warm red mixture to paint spirals, turtles, and other designs on his chest, face, arms, and thighs.

Redbone used a hafted rock hoe to dig a shallow grave and gathered enough rocks to bury their friend's body deep enough to keep scavengers from digging it up. He oriented the grave so that the dead man's body soul could see the rising sun.

They wrapped the prepared body in a deer hide blanket and carried it to the grave. While Redbone laid the body reverently in the grave and began placing dirt and rocks over it, Red Petal chanted a death song and prayers to guide Hawkeye's spirit to the Land of the Ancestors.

When all was done, Red Petal's tears were over. She took Redbone's hand, pulled him up, and kissed him on the cheek.

"Thank you," she said. Looking him in the eye with a slight smile, "Now, come make love to me."

They walked slowly back to the shelter holding hands, both wondering what would happen next.

CHAPTER 16

MARRIED

The Green Corn Celebration had come and gone, leaves on the deciduous trees were beginning to change to their autumn hues, and the nights had lost their summer heat and humidity by the time Redbone and Red Petal glided into the New Long Pine Village canoe landing.

"Blue Deer has changed a great deal in appearance!" Bright Moon called to the approaching canoe. She was dressed in the red shirt of a deputy war chief. Her hair was in a single braid down the middle between her shoulder blades. Her temples sported two new cattail tattoos.

"Looks as if you have been busy yourself, little sister," he chided.

"There are stories to tell." She looked at a handful of warriors who seemed to be with her. "Carry their packs to the Water Plant Clan longhouse. And be careful. I am sure my brother has some valuable trade goods in those packs."

"Yes, Deputy," six warriors answered in unison.

"Sounds like you have them trained well!"

"Due respect, trader," one of the warriors told Redbone in a warning tone.

Redbone nodded as he climbed out of the canoe and stepped forward to help Red Petal. She was already standing in front of Bright Moon when he hobbled up.

"I am Red Petal, Redbone's friend from Sun Town." She held out a hand, palm up.

"I think you gathered that I am Bright Moon, Redbone's little sister." She returned the greeting gesture.

The only thing little about Bright Moon was her waist. Even in a war shirt, her muscular arms and shoulders were evident. She was taller than Redbone, and her legs provided a strong foundation. Her facial structure was similar to Redbone's. She was a real beauty. But her expression said she lived by her own rules. Red Petal was duly impressed.

In the days after Hawkeye's funeral, Red Petal put her soul and body into helping Redbone get their canoe and packs over the mountains to the Ohi-yo River. She had developed her own powerful muscles and stamina. Bright Moon immediately approved of her as a suitable partner for her brother. They were obviously more than friends.

"Let me show you to the Water Plant Clan longhouse. We will do formal introductions there," Bright Moon told Red Petal, ignoring Redbone. He followed along, noting his sister may have found a lifelong friend.

Ducking through the elk hide door hanging, the warm big room felt good on the cool afternoon. Red Petal did not know what to expect, but seeing the squat, oval-shaped buildings in this village took her by surprise. Though the building techniques were similar, the shape of the buildings seemed strange to her.

They came to a long central firepit with several people present. A woman who looked too young to sit at the head of the fire jumped up and walked quickly to Redbone and wrapped him in a big hug.

"Welcome home, son! You are home early. I am sure you have much to tell us." She stepped back and looked him over from head to toe. If anything, he looked a little bigger and much stronger than when he left. "You do not look any worse for the wear."

"Good to be home, Mother. Some introductions are in order."

She looked at Red Petal and did a double take. "I am sorry, maiden. I was expecting Blue Deer and did not look closely. My mistake! Yes, let us get to the introductions. Come sit by me, maiden."

At Bright Star's invitation, Red Petal sat to her left, then Redbone, then Bright Moon. To the right of Bright Star sat Red Hand, Water Mint, Tallow, Wise Beaver and his wife Silver Star, Snow Lily and her husband Green Hawk, and Oak Shield, still single.

"I will introduce every one of the locals, then Redbone can introduce our special guest. Does that sound amenable to all of you?" Bright Moon asked.

All heads nodded. No one was about to counter the Head Matron. It took Bright Star more than a finger of time to list the positions, clans, and lineages of each person around the firepit. When she finished, she deferred to Redbone.

Redbone stood and signaled Red Petal to stand. "It is my pleasure to introduce my soon-to-be wife, Red Petal of the Turtle Clan…" He listed all the family, clan, people, and village information about her. She stood blushing.

"We are pleased to welcome you to our family," Bright Star said to Red Petal.

"It is my honor to meet the people who raised such a strong and noble son, whom I have witnessed act with honor in a variety of situations. It is an honor and a privilege for this maiden to be invited into a family who has raised such a fine son." Now Redbone was blushing.

Everyone raised a hand. "Greetings, Red Petal!"

Right after Red Petal and Redbone sat back down, bowls of venison stew and honey-flavored acorn cakes were served.

When the bowls were collected and tea cups refilled, Bright Star asked Redbone to start the story-telling. The story about finding Yellow Hair's plank left Bright Star visibly shaken. But the story of fleeing Willet Village and self-imposed exile, the death of a close friend, and falling in love left everyone stunned.

"We will talk more of these things," a shocked Bright Star said quietly.

"What are your plans? When do you plan your wedding?" Bright Star looked at Redbone, but her eyes shifted from his to Red Petal's.

"As soon as possible for the wedding. Right after the snow melt flooding, we plan a trading venture to Cahokia. Of course, I want to see Traveler before winter sets in here."

"What of Red Petal's family? Will you be married in Sun Town? Will they venture here? Are you taking her on your trade to Cahokia? So many questions." Bright Star was too flustered to think.

"No. We want just a small, private wedding. Her family is a long story that we will tell as we go along. To answer your question, we are partners and will face any and all hardships together. She will go where I go, and I will go where she wishes me to take her. If you are concerned about children, there probably will never be any."

"Can you two stay and talk privately with me?" Bright Star asked.

"We have nowhere else to go."

"The rest of you, please leave us," said Bright Star.

"Can I stay, brother? I want to hear this," Bright Moon teased.

"What do you think?" Redbone asked Red Petal.

"I think everyone is going to hear it all sooner or later. I have no secrets anymore."

"I guess anyone who wants to stay is welcome for our purposes."

"I will stay, but the rest of my family will take their leave, now." Water Mint was very curious, but as Head Matron of the Water Plant Clan, she felt it was her duty to hear.

"All right, we will have myself, Water Mint, Red Hand, Bright Moon, Redbone, and Red Petal in attendance to hear Redbone's story about Red Petal's history. See that we are not disturbed," Bright Star announced, eyes boring into Tallow's.

Tallow led the rest of his family to their family chambers further down the longhouse.

"What do you need to tell us, Redbone?" Bright Star queried.

"It started ten-and-eight sun cycles past..."

Redbone told of the actions that made his deceased friend a member of the Turkey Clan in Willet Village, how Strong Wing met up with and married Red Petal's mother, how Red Petal and Strong Wing's brother always had a special relationship and when they reached adulthood, had fallen in love. By the laws of the Lenape, Red Petal and the dead young man were too closely related to marry. In a strictly technical sense, they were not related because Strong Wing's Brother shared no blood with anyone in the Turkey Clan. The boy was not even adopted by the clan. He was bought and given an assumed identity, but no formal adoption was ever made. Redbone asserted that was why he agreed to bring the lovers to New Long Pine Village. No Lenape clan laws would affect them here. That the young man died, presumably by a spider bite, opened the door for Redbone and Red Petal to fall in love. They could not go back to Sun Town or Willet Village because the ensuing scandal would destroy the leadership structure of Willet Village and have a negative impact on the Turtle Clan in Sun Town. The falling game pieces could destroy the entire River Lenape network. For everyone's sake, it is better for Red Petal to simply disappear from that network.

"Does this make sense?" Redbone finished his long narration.

"Brother, you sure know how to kick a hornet's nest!" Bright Moon remarked.

"Red Petal, are you sure you are ready to forsake your heritage? Never see any of them again?" Bright Star asked.

"My place is with the man I love, wherever that takes me, Head Matron," Red Petal replied honestly.

"She sounds exactly like the older Bright Moon when she followed Yellow Hair into the unknown," said Water Mint.

"Do you think anyone from Sun Town or Willet

Village will come looking for you?" Bright Star asked Red Petal.

"I seriously doubt it. The villages are all under threat from the Great Crab Bay alliance to the south and the Minquas, what you call Haudenosaunee, to the north. They need to keep as many warriors home as they can."

"And if someone did come looking for you, what would you do?"

"I would consult with my husband, and we would reach a decision together. Honestly, I think of going back into that cauldron of backstabbing corrupt politics, and I cringe. I can think of no freer way to live than with my man on the rivers."

Redbone turned to Red Petal and said, "I love you."

She smiled and squeezed the hand she had been holding since the conversation began.

"What are your thoughts on this matter, Red Hand?" Bright Star asked.

"Like our daughter said—our son sure kicked a hornet's nest. I do not see a 'fix' to the mess until all of the people involved pass from the scene. By then, a new hornet's nest will no doubt replace this one. You may recall, we had our own hornet's nest right in this valley, not so many sun cycles past. It took a woman of remarkable skill and determination to fix that mess."

Bright Star sat staring at nothing as a tear trickled down her cheek.

"Perhaps we have talked enough for this night. I think we should retire to our chambers. Redbone, your chamber is ready for you and Red Petal. Tomorrow, we can discuss your wedding," Bright Star said.

"And I wish to hear my sister's stories as well," Redbone replied.

"Not much to tell. Someone came along looking for a fight. I showed him one. He will never reach his ancestors."

———

With mixed emotions, ten days after Redbone returned from his first trading adventure, Bright Star hosted the marriage between Red Petal and her son. There were few guests beyond immediate family, and the bride had no family at all.

Redbone determined the best action they could take was trip downriver to Monongahela Village. He wanted to see Traveler and tell him about his experiences in Willet Village. Of course, the big news was Red Petal. Traveler might remember her, but she was too young to remember his brief appearance in her life.

The morning after the small wedding, Redbone and Red Petal loaded some personal gear and a few trade goods into Redbone's bark canoe. It was the first bark canoe she had ever been in. At first, she thought it was too wobbly, but she quickly adapted and became efficient in working with Redbone directing the craft where they wanted it to go.

Each night they would stop early to make sure they had enough time to set up a snug camp. The nights ranged from cold to freezing. A blazing camp-fire was a must. Redbone brought a bear skin for their bed and elk skins for blankets. They would spend long nights naked in those skins, and he wanted his bride as comfortable as he could make her.

Strong Elk greeted them on the river before they got to the Monongahela Village canoe landing.

"You have certainly improved the company you keep since last you arrived at this landing," Strong Elk teased.

"Your manners have not! Is that any way to address a newly married woman?" Redbone returned.

"Where is her husband?"

Red Petal laughed out loud at Strong Elk's banter.

"Welcome to Monongahela Village, my lady. Maybe we can find you some more worthy company than a river trader. Perhaps a deputy war chief would better suit your needs."

"No wonder you are still a bachelor, Strong Elk. You have the manners of packrat marooned on an island."

"Well, if all you are going to do is insult me, I will dismiss my patrol, and you can carry your own packs to Corn Silk's longhouse." Strong Elk kept the banter going as long as the young woman was smiling.

"I call a truce, cousin. This beautiful maid is Red Petal, wife of Redbone. We greet you with friendship and wishes of good health. May the heavy snows of winter avoid your lodge, your larder always remain full, and your company hearty."

"You have come to the right place for full larders, cousin. Our crops may have been the biggest ever, and the deer are practically running into the village begging to be shot. Come, let us find a warmer place to make small talk."

There was no snow on the ground, but the air felt cold enough, even though the wispy clouds foretold of no impending storms. The group of warriors followed them through the turns of the palisade entrance and to the east end of the Corn Clan longhouse. Once they entered the big room, it took a few heartbeats for their eyes to adjust. The heat was almost overwhelming after spending the first half of the day on the cold river.

Redbone smiled when he saw Traveler sitting in his special seat with the backrest covered with a mountain lion skin. He took Red Petal's hand and walked over beside the elder.

"Greetings, Elder. Redbone has returned from the lands of the Lenape with a wife. Red Petal, I am honored to reintroduce you to the great trader, Traveler. He claims no clan but has been adopted into the Corn Clan in Monongahela Village. Traveler, I am honored to reintroduce you to Red Petal of the Round Shell Lineage of the Turtle Clan of the Turtle People of Sun Town in the Lenni Lenape Nation."

"Ah, she was but a small child when I last saw this one. Petal, was it? Just as pretty now as then, I might add." Traveler laughed as he studied her features. "Yes, child, you are the image of your mother."

"Honored to meet you, Grandfather. I am afraid you have the advantage on me. I was too young, and I am afraid I do not remember you."

"Of course not. I was a dashing and handsome man in those days, not the dried-up, toothless old husk you see today. Forgive me if I do not stand up. My knees, they do not like to support me any longer."

Redbone and Red Petal stayed four days in Monongahela Village. The story of Yellow Hair's plank brought a tear to Traveler's eyes. Redbone noted further deterioration of Traveler's physical condition. He had difficulty walking without a walking stick and needed help getting up and down, his eyes were slowly covering with gray crystals, and his hearing was beginning to fail. His hair was reduced to a few wispy tufts above his large ears. His skin was a network of creases and wrinkles and was covered with random brown spots. The joint stiffening disease had made his hands knobby and uncoordinated. But his mind was remarkably intact. He could remember events and stories from his long life as if he lived them yesterday.

Despite Traveler's failing health, Redbone and he shared meaningful conversations about travel on the Spirit, Grandfather, and Grandmother rivers. Redbone hoped to see the Shining Mountains before returning to New Long Pine Village. He also promised Traveler he and Red Petal would stop at Monongahela Village on their way west in the spring.

"Are you sure you wish to bring your woman on such an arduous adventure? There are those who will want to take her and leave you dead," Traveler warned the young man but knew he would not change his mind.

The return trip to New Long Pine Village was colder than the trip downriver had been. For one thing, each day they were paddling into a blustery northwest wind. Wolf-skin hoods and elk robes helped, but the biting wind stung their eyes and any exposed skin.

The river was virtually covered with ducks and geese. Each night and every morning they dined on fresh roasted, fried, or stewed waterfowl of one form or another. Redbone marveled that there were so many of the birds. He could not help but wonder where they all came from.

The last night on the river, they lay snugged in their elk sleeping blanket. Their bodies were wet with sweat after vigorous lovemaking. He held her warm body tightly to his own. *Every day I thank the creator for bringing this perfect woman to me. I feel bad for what happened to her first man, but it feels so right. She learned the Monongahela tongue like she was born to it. I started teaching them as soon as we left Willet Village. And after our friend lost his life, she insisted we only talk in my people's tongue. By the time we reached New Long Pine Village, she could use it as well as me. It is as if we were made for each other.*

"What is it, husband? You seem distracted."

"Just thinking how lucky I am that we are together."

"I liked and admired you very much. But that first time, when our deceased friend told us to couple, I knew I would love you for the rest of my days. We fit so perfectly, physically, and are souls are locked together. I do not know how to explain it, but I know what I feel...and what I see in your eyes—even when it is too dark to see. Thank you for taking me away from my old life."

Her thigh felt a slight arousal in his soft manhood. That triggered another round of passion. Lying there, catching their breath in the warm blankets, Traveler's warning came to Redbone's mind.

"Are you absolutely certain you wish to go west with me? I worry about Traveler's words. He carries much wisdom in that old brain of his. He told me there are men in the wilder parts of the world who would take you from me and leave me dead. I could not stand to see you dragged away from me. You can be assured that I would fight to my death to protect you. But I know I can be overpowered, and that worries me." Redbone pulled her closer to him.

"And you can rest assured, my husband, I will die before any person, or wild animal drags me away from you." She pushed herself tight into his body.

They slept dreamlessly until the noisy waterfowl on the river brought them awake after light had returned to the valley.

"I guess we should get moving," Redbone said.

"Not until you warm my body—from the inside." She slid her hand across his manhood and kissed his neck.

"I could never refuse that order, my beautiful wife." His response was rapid, as was hers.

The sun was well up before they were underway after a morning meal of hot duck stew and spruce needle tea. It took them most of a hand of time to pack away their camp, their chores being interrupted with kisses every time they crossed paths. It was by no accident that happened frequently.

The couple was warmly greeted in New Long Pine Village. The village was actively engaged in preparing for the coming winter. Piles of leaves that had collected inside the palisade were pulled away from the walls and pushed into heaps on bare ground. Those heaps were burned to get rid of the fire hazard along the walls and other structures. Small children took advantage of the heaped leaves and made a game of running and jumping into the soft masses before the adults could start the fires.

Many warriors were afield hunting all the deer, elk, and moose they could find to provide winter food. Adolescents were out gathering nuts and acorns. Women were collecting reeds and cattails for weaving baskets and mats. All of the crops had been harvested, but some women were busy pounding corn in log mortars to make cornmeal. Others were taking dried beans from racks and putting them in baked clay storage vessels.

A group of men were busy making repairs to longhouses that needed a slab of bark or tie-down saplings replaced. Still others were building racks for smoking the meat hunters would be bringing in.

Few elders were out and about. They were in warm longhouses sitting by firepits, smoking clay pipes, discussing how bad the winter would be and comparing current conditions with those of the past. Sharp criticism was common about the way the younger people were preparing for winter compared to how it was done in sun cycles gone by.

Once they were settled in, Redbone and Red Petal joined one group or another to complete this task or that one. The village was prepared for winter before the first snow fell.

With most of the work for winter preparations completed, Redbone managed to catch Bright Moon before she left to go hunting one morning.

"Sister, I wonder if you might be able to squeeze in some time to teach Red Petal how to defend herself."

"It would be my pleasure to teach my sister some fighting skills. You should be more careful what you ask for, brother."

"Why do you say that?"

"Because, when I am finished with her, she will be able to twist you like a knot of tobacco."

"Good. Traveler tells me that where we will be going next trading season, there may be some rough men who could take her and leave me dead. I want her to be able to defend herself."

"In a fight, there are no guarantees, but it always helps if you know how to hurt people. I will show her some tricks I have learned. And then, she can teach you. When do you want me to start?"

"I will let you two work that out."

"Where is she?"

"Helping Mother distribute corn meal to the different clans. They should be back soon."

"All right, I will wait here. So, tell me. This man that died, was it really a spider bite, or did you have to kill him, and that story about the spider bite was just a cover? Spider bites can be, but they are rarely, fatal."

"No! Well, I think it was a spider bit. It was high on his neck, right at the base of his skull. I think the venom went into his brain. He acted very strangely. His souls went loose. He was angry all the time. He claimed he and Red Petal were married, and he had the right to do anything he wanted to her. I told him if he hurt her in any way, we would have trouble.

Shortly after that is when he attacked me, broke his arm, and hit his head. His souls wandered from his body more than two hands of time."

"That is a strange case. You may be right about the venom getting into his brain. Did he have a fever?"

"I noticed he was a little warm when I was setting his arm. After his souls returned to his body, he would not let either of us touch him."

"He must have known he was dying and, in his sick state of mind, did not want you feeling sorry for him."

"That is what Red Petal thought after he died."

"Interesting."

Bright Star and Red Petal came through the door hanging and walked over to them. "Talking about us?" Red Petal asked coyly.

"Yes we were. I am going to teach you how to defend yourself from predators, like my brother." Bright Moon smiled mischievously as she looked from face to face.

"He may have his faults, but I would not call him a predator," Bright Star joined the conversation.

"Not fair, I am outnumbered," Redbone declared.

"Just wait until I get you one on one!" Red Petal added.

"Girls, you go somewhere and practice your fighting. I wish to have words with my son," Bright Star declared.

The questions revolved around how Redbone

intended to keep his wife safe from bad men and wild animals in the far-off lands he intended to go trading in. After a lengthy discussion Bright Star resigned to the fact that there were never guarantees. Accidents, bad men, and vicious animals can show up anywhere, anytime.

Winter came and brought heavy snows, thaws, and more snows. When all was said and done, it was a typical winter. They were prepared and still food stores began to run low after the spring equinox, just like always. Bright Moon and Red Petal became fast friends and hunting partners. Redbone was left behind most days when the girls went in search of game. He, Tallow, and Red Hand hunted together frequently, but did not bring in the number of carcasses the girls did. No one in the village could match Bright Moon's hunting skills.

With spring finally making an appearance, Redbone and Red Petal began making preparations for their trading excursion into the west. Redbone estimated they would be gone four or five sun cycles. They would live off their wits and skills honed in the forests over the winter.

The warm up brought heavy rains and snowmelt, causing major flooding in the Ohi-yo Valley, all its tributaries, and all the major rivers. Travel would have to wait until the flooding subsided. The Planting Moon was nearly at an end when the rivers were finally navigable.

Redbone and Red Petal still acted like newlyweds

on their nuptial deer hunt. Redbone was worried he would run out of squawroot before he could find some new plants growing. It turned out that Bright Moon knew exactly when and where to find new shoots peeping through the spring soil.

When the day of departure was finally upon them, many villagers went to the canoe landing to watch the heavily laden bark canoe set out down-river. Many hugs and tears were spent on the farewell.

"Someone I love is always leaving me," Bright Star sobbed. Her attachment to her son and his bride was evident to all.

Bright Moon's goodbye was a bit more brief. A quick hug, and, "Take care, you hear?". It was more an order than a question.

Red Hand shook hands, hugged and kissed Red Petal on the cheek, then bearhugged Redbone and said he was proud of him.

Finally, they shoved off into an uncharted future.

CHAPTER 17
RIVERS

Though the Ohi-yo was well within its banks, it still carried a higher than normal flow, the current fast and unpredictable. The two and a half-day float to the mouth of the Kiskiminetas tested their skills and endurance. They arrived and set up their camp well before sunset. They noted someone had already camped there before them this season.

Redbone set about putting up their conical tent using green cedar poles he cut from the local area. While he was occupied with putting up their shelter, Red Petal brought an ample supply of firewood to the recently used fire ring and got a fire started. Soon she had a bag on a tripod heating water for spruce needle tea. She also had two ducks plucked and rubbed with fat stuck on stout willow branches ready to set over hot coal.

The weather was pleasant, so while Redbone was

finishing with the tent, complete with bedrolls and clean clothes for the morning float to Monongahela Village, she slipped out of her clothing and sat facing him in a provocative pose.

When he walked out of the tent for the last time, he looked at her.

"Now, that is just not fair!" As he began stripping as fast as he could.

While he was ripping his clothes off, she spread the blanket she was hiding, lay on her back, and splayed her legs apart. By the time he laid down next to her, he was ready for action. After a frantic coupling, they lay snuggled together in the warm, late afternoon sun.

"Can I make evening meal now?" she asked innocently.

"You started this," he retorted.

"I never said a word."

"Not with your tongue!"

"Hmm, I thought I used my tongue plenty!"

"Well, not for talking, anyway."

The next morning after duck meat in corn gruel, they packed for the short float to Monongahela Village. Redbone was worried they would find that Traveler had died over the winter.

Red Petal was somewhat worried when she saw the turbulence where the Monongahela and Ohi-yo Rivers came together. *When we came in the fall, the meeting of the waters was not nearly this violent. I am not sure I can survive that!*

"Turn upriver! Follow the north bank, and we will soon come to a place to cross!" Redbone had to shout to be heard, but she caught on, and they were soon on the south side approaching the canoe landing.

They found an opening in the long row of over-turned canoes along the bank. The canoes lay on the bank with only the longer dugout bows poking above the top. Redbone did not notice any with trader emblems painted on their bows.

Redbone was disappointed when a band of warriors trotted down the path from the village, but Strong Elk was not among them.

"Greetings, trader. I am Moose Eater, warrior of the Deer Clan. My men will carry your packs to a storage area in the Corn Clan longhouse. Strong Elk sends his greeting but was unable to come out here. He has a broken leg and is not able to get around on his crutch very well."

"My wife, Red Petal, and Redbone are honored to meet you, Moose Eater. Sometime, I think I would like to hear the story of how you came by that name." Redbone grinned to his wife while he dreamed up various scenarios.

"Not nearly as interesting as your imagination, Redbone. When I was a young adolescent, my father killed a moose and brought it to our lodge. We lived in Riverbirch Village. It was my first taste of moose meat. I kept sneaking pieces of the tasty meat, and my father took to calling me 'Moose Eater.' The shaman thought the name was appropriate and gave me that name at my naming ceremony."

"Still a good story." Redbone shouldered a pack with some of their personal things, took Red Petal's hand, and started for the palisade.

"Can you say if the elder trader is still among the living?" Redbone could not contain his curiosity.

"Traveler? Yes, he still sits on his seat and tells stories to anyone who will listen. I can say he is looking forward to your arrival."

Redbone squeezed Red Petal's hand and gave her a smile, which she returned. Bright Star and Bright Moon had told her that Redbone worshipped Traveler since he had seen three moons.

It was late morning when Redbone saw Traveler sitting on his seat with the mountain lion hide back-rest. The first thing he notice was that Traveler's pupils were completely covered with a glassy gray film. He was obviously blind.

"Greetings, Traveler, we are back. My heart sings to see you!" said Redbone.

"Who said that? Is that you, Redbone? I cannot see more than a few shadows, and my ears mostly hear insects buzzing, but my heart sings to hear your voice. You wintered better than I, I trust. That pretty wife of yours is with you. I can smell something pretty, and I know it is not you."

"You flatter me, Grandfather. I fear I smell like the river we have been on for four days. Perhaps that is what you smell."

"Ah, and your voice is like the lark singing. Does your husband say nice things like that to you?" Traveler joked.

"He does, but it is usually other, physical attributes he compliments." She tried to keep up with Traveler's humor.

"Yes, young men think with their...well, not their brains."

Corn Silk came into the room. She was dressed in a drab, brown doeskin dress with a corn ear and leaf painted on the front. Her gray-streaked hair was plaited in a single braid that trailed partway down her back.

"I thought I heard a female voice in here. Greetings, young maid. I pray you are well today, Red Petal. Though I pity you for spending so much time in the company of men." She waved her hand to indicate everyone else in the room was male.

"It keeps me on my toes, Head Matron. It appears things are well in the village. You wintered well?" Red Petal asked.

"Yes, most things are fine, and our problems are minor. Thank you for asking. You are very polite for one so young."

"Manners were part of my upbringing, Head Matron. My great-grandmother and grandmother were Great Sakimaxkwe of the River Lenape People."

"And here you are, plying rivers in the company of traders. That must be a long story, but I will not trouble you to recite it here. If you are happy, that is what counts."

"I could not be happier, Head Matron."

"I pray your happiness lasts. I must go now. Enjoy your stay." Corn Silk waved a hand to the others, turned, and walked to another part of the longhouse.

"How is your grandmother handling her responsibilities, Red Petal?" Traveler asked.

"She is getting by, but she is not the leader my great-grandmother was. I think my mother will be better if the Council of Elders do not remove my grandmother and select another clan to lead our people."

"Do you aspire to that position?"

"Certainly not. I am here because I am not built to conform to all those clan laws and rules. I aim to be free like you were most of your days."

"Ha, and you are dragging your man along, so you need not worry about meeting some handsome war chief to suck you into clan duties and responsibilities." Traveler chuckled at his witticism.

"Exactly." She looked at Redbone and smiled as he shook his head.

The conversation and bantering was interrupted when two servants brought in some corn cakes with dried blueberries and sassafras tea for everyone. Traveler fell asleep and began snoring loudly after eating half of one of the small cakes.

Redbone was going to suggest that he and Red

Petal get settled into their sleeping chamber when Strong Elk came hobbling in on a crutch with his left leg splinted and wrapped from the knee down. A pretty young maiden walked right behind him.

"Greetings, Strong Elk. It seems I have fared better this past winter than you."

"Not sure I would say that. Yellow Flower has made me a happy man. Oh, you mean the leg. That was Yellow Flower too. In fact, that is how we met. I was walking by the Deer Clan longhouse one cold day early in the Awakening Moon. Yellow Flower came out and said her roof was leaking and all the Deer Clan warriors were either on patrol or out hunting. I went in to see what the problem was and could see a slab of the roof bark was split."

"Being and honorable man, you offered to fix her roof," said Redbone.

"Exactly. I found a suitable sized slab stored in that longhouse. Taking my knife and plenty of cord, I climbed up onto the roof where the bad slab was. I quickly had the old bark off and made the repair. I got everything tied down and had done a good job if I say so, myself. I started back down. Did I mention it was cold?"

"I believe you did," Redbone chided.

"Well, it was freezing. On my way down I slipped on some hidden ice on one of the tie-down saplings. I lost my balance and tumble down off the roof. My foot caught between the lowest tie-down sapling and the bark wall. It happened to be right where the bark slab was attached to an inner support pole. Those things have no give to them. So, as you can see, my leg did give and snapped the two bones in my lower leg."

"Sounds painful," Red Petal offered.

Strong Elk just looked at her, then continued. "Yellow Flower, sweetheart that she is, ran and got the Deer Clan healer. He found two Hawk Clan warriors, and they got me out of there and carried me to the healer's lodge. It took all three of them to set my broken bones. I think I was delirious with the pain. Sometime later, I woke up to see this sweet face looking at me, waiting for my souls to return."

"How nice," Red Petal said to Yellow Flower.

"I felt responsible for all his pain," Yellow Flower said in a sweet voice.

"She felt so sorry for me, she offered to marry me. How could I feel any pain after that? Her father made this crutch for me, and I have been hobbling around ever since. At least I missed being on patrol in the wet, sloppy Awakening Moon."

"Will it heal so you can walk normal?" Redbone asked.

"The healer, End of Storm, says it should heal fine, but I could always have a little limp. You know how that is, Redbone."

Redbone and Red Petal stayed in Monongahela three more days. Each day they talked to Traveler, Corn Silk, War Chief Snarling Wolf, Strong Elk, and Yellow Flower.

With enough dried and jerked deer, elk, and turkey to last two moons, they started down the Spirit River. They would take it to the grandfather and follow it six days to Cahokia. There, they hoped to find a guide, or at least instructions for how to move up the Grandmother River to the Shining Mountains.

Redbone followed Traveler's suggestions to travel by day until they reached Squirreltail Village. They found the old leaders of the village had gone on to the afterlife and new leadership was in charge. In spite of the changes, they made some good trades and slept on a warm pallet for a change.

Redbone declared they would travel only in the darkness until they were close to the Grandfather River to avoid contact with the warlike Illini people. They pulled away from the Squirreltail canoe landing as the sun set in an orange sky. Slowly, their eyes adjusted as darkness descended upon them on the lonely river. Red Petal found she was able to read the currents, snags, and sawyers better than anticipated. The starlight reflected off every irregularity on the surface. She could almost read the river better than in the daylight.

When the first hint of light foretold the coming of a new day, they searched and found a creek on the south bank to hide their canoe. The plan was not to put up any shelter that might betray their location. Instead, the couple sought small thickets that would hide their bedrolls and sleeping bodies from any patrols out on the water.

After the requisite lovemaking, both drifted into a deep sleep in the dark shadows of their thicket. Just after sunset, Redbone awoke to the call of a barred owl.

"Kicking us out of our shelter, friend?" Redbone said quietly.

Red Petal sat up so fast, she was dizzy. "Who were you talking to?" she asked, a bewildered look on her face as she searched her surroundings.

"Just an owl that was perched over our heads until you moved so quickly."

For several days their routine was the same—wake up at dusk, eat a cold meal, get on the river a hand after dark, float and paddle along the south riverbank until the faintest hint of a new day shown in the black sky if it was cloudy, or the weakest stars began to fade, camp along some obscure creek, make love, go to sleep, repeat.

Few settlements or individual farms dotted the south side of the river. The north side was home to some people, for there were occasional lights from campfires, including a few clusters of them. More often, there was a glow of many fires hidden by a palisade wall. Redbone's plan was to avoid people until they reached the Grandfather River.

———

BEAR HUNTER HAD SEEN two-tens of summers. He was leading a party of six young warriors along the south side of the Spirit River three days east of their village. Big Bear Village was one of the few villages on the south side of the wide river.

What is this? He bent down and studied the shallow footprint. At least he thought it was a foot-print. *It is too small for a man, and too far from the village to be one of our women.* He searched and could not find another anywhere around.

"Looks Wide, come here!" he called to his closest companion.

"What have you found, Bear Hunter?" Looks Wide asked as he trotted up. Bear Hunter motioned him to be quiet and to be careful where he stepped.

"It is a woman's track, I think, but I can find no other. Help me search." The two started a systematic search of the area. The others joined them, and Bear Hunter sent them along a small creek that flowed toward the river.

Soon, the yip of a fox came from the creek close to the river.

"See here, Bear Hunter. A canoe was landed here yesterday, I would say, then pulled out last night. Probably traders, I would guess. Most likely harm-less. Maybe we will catch them in the village. But here is the strange part. One is a big man with a bad foot, the other is a woman. Look at these tracks." Otter showed Bear Hunter the unusual track of the man with what looked like a club foot.

"The woman wears an unusual style of moccasin. I have never seen one this style," Otter said, looking around for confirmation.

"I have. It comes from the Lenni Lenape Village in Sun Town across the eastern mountains," offered Five Kills, a seasoned older warrior from the Wolf Clan.

"Where?" demanded Bear Hunter.

"Many sun cycles past, we caught some traders trying to sneak through our lands, just like these two. We had four canoes of five warriors each. I was in the last canoe. Our leaders ran them to ground five days west of here. The hot head leading the fight did not organize, and those traders, there was two men and a woman, cut our warriors down like spring grass, and escaped. Ten of us cut through the forest to hit their back side. They were waiting and killed five before they got back to their canoe and escaped. We got to the bank and launched arrows at them, but they were out of range before we could do any damage. Then, we had wounded to care for, and those traders got away. One of them was that Yellow Hair snake, and that woman was the fiercest fighter among them, if the wounded men could be believed."

"I remember hearing that story. No one pursued them?" Bear Hunter asked.

"Of course we did. But the trail was cold, and we never found them."

"We will not let that happen again. We must run back to the village, get canoes, and search every tree, every reed, every blade of grass until we find them. We will make them pay for what those others did then," Bear Hunter declaration, proud of himself.

"That is a foolish plan if I ever heard one," said Five Kills.

"How so?"

"To catch them, we need to take one canoe, travel at night, like them, and catch them when they hole up for the day. The fewer we take, the better our chances. More warriors means more noise to alert them. Stealth will get our prey. After we kill the man, we use the woman until we tire of her, then kill her."

"Who do you propose goes on this hunt?"

"The five of us know about it. Let us go get a canoe. We need not tell anyone else what we are up to."

Thinking about using the woman, Otter said, "I am in!"

Soon they were in a distance-eating trot for Big Bear Village. With few stops to catch their breath, have a bite of pemican or jerky, and a swallow of water, they were at the Big Bear canoe landing four hands of time before sunup the following night. After replenishing their pemican and jerky supplies, they were on the river before the village began to stir.

As they stroked their paddles for maximum speed while conserving as much energy as possible, they had no idea they were gaining on their prey rapidly.

REDBONE AND RED PETAL continued their routine, not knowing they were being hunted by a group of predators looking for easy prey. When the first hints of a new day shone in the heavens, they found a suitable creek and eased into it. The cautious couple had managed to slip by a large village on the south side of the river by drifting away to the dark north side until the village was out of sight.

"I think we should start posting a guard while the other sleeps starting today," Redbone offered.

"Good idea. You sleep first. I am not sleepy right now."

"See that white cedar thicket? From there, you can see the creek channel and have a good view of which one of us is sleeping. If you want first guard duty, it is yours. Can you do a good bluejay call? They are common enough, and active all day long."

She answered in a bluejay scolding call that elicited an answer from a wild bird five tens of paces away.

"That will do," he said before stretching out on his bedroll hidden in cluster of chestnut saplings sprouting from the rotted bole of an old tree that had died several sun cycles past.

Red Petal took her bow she and Bright Moon had crafted, and a quiver of arrows. She checked her warclub, three bone stilettoes, and her hafted flint knife. All were handy and ready for use. She found that from the thicket, she could stand on her knees and see her husband clearly, and the channel from the river to their canoe. She was ready.

The sun was nearly halfway to its zenith in the sky when a movement on the river got her attention. It was a canoe with six warriors coming straight for their creek channel.

She gave out her bluejay call. The warriors looked her way but saw nothing but a bluejay flying up to a higher limb in a big cottonwood tree several paces behind her. She saw Redbone look her way. She pointed toward the creek and signaled him to stay down.

The canoe started up the narrow channel. One of the warriors pointed into the water like he was seeing something. She realized they had pushed their paddles into the mud as they moved along in the shallow water. After the muddy water settled, the holes were left in the mud. They were found. The warriors were quietly stringing their bows.

Do I warn them, or just shoot to kill? They look like a rough bunch, and I doubt they will give us a chance. Still...

"All right, you know we are here. You have arrows pointed at you. Are you going to leave and let us pass? Or do you wish to die?" she called.

The one in front was the only one with a nocked arrow at that moment.

"You are only a girl. I plan to have my way with you, as do all my warriors!" They did not know where Redbone was yet. The man started to raise his bow toward her.

Her arrow slammed into his chest just to the left of his sternum. The impact took his breath, and the bloody point protruded from his back.

"Get her," the others yelled in unison.

But she disappeared as she ducked and nocked her second arrow. Four arrows flew over her back. She rose and shot her next arrow into the second man in the canoe as he was attempting to climb out.

Redbone's first arrow struck down a warrior who had stepped out of the canoe, but his foot was mired in the thick mud next to the canoe, and he could not move fast enough to get away from the projectile. The fourth man was running straight at Red Petal with a drawn war club. She had time to get another shot off, but decided to meet him with her war club, using the training Bright Moon had given her.

She stepped out of her thicket and avoided his club as it swished over her head. Her counter-swing came up between his legs and smashed into his groin. His breechclout did nothing to soften the blow. He dropped to his knees and screamed until vomit filled his mouth. Otter knew he would die before he would take the girl. She left him and went to aid Redbone, who was in trouble.

The fifth warrior in the fight was the grizzled older man. He ran to attack Redbone. He faked a swing at Redbone's head and swung his club down in a circle move that Redbone deflected, but the impact bruised his arm deeply.

The sixth warrior lay slumped in their canoe with one of Red Petal's arrows through his chest.

Thinking he had won; the warrior raised his club to finish his adversary. A sharp pain in his back ended his joy. Red Petal's club bashed into Five Kill's spine between his shoulder blades. The impact severed his spinal cord, and he fell in a heap, stunned and unable to move or feel pain. He was, however, very much aware that he was defeated and about to die.

Redbone used his club to end Five Kills's misery.

"Any more left alive?" Redbone winced, his arm obviously causing him much pain.

"One more laying in the leaves over there with no more functioning man parts," said Red Petal proudly, adrenaline coursing through her body.

"Is your arm broken?" she asked as she tenderly felt the big red spot.

"No, I do not think so. Just bruised all the way to the bone."

"Let us see if we can get any information from that one." She indicated the warrior still writhing in the old leaves on the forest floor.

"You sit on that fallen tree. I will question our friend here." She pointed to the log, then to the quivering young warrior.

Red Petal bent down to talk to the wounded man. She noted the proximity to the vomit, grabbed the man's breechclout and dragged him a few paces away.

"Talk to me, boy," she ordered the hapless warrior. He gave her a worried look.

"It can be easy, or you can make it hard. Are there any more coming after us?"

He shook his head but did not speak.

"Where are you from?"

Silence.

"Where are you from?" She stood and took a step toward his waist, fists knotted.

"Bi'B...bar Village," he mumbled.

"Big Bear Village?" she asked, and he nodded his head.

"Are there more coming after us?"

"I don' tink so," was the best he could do. He lay his head down and panted for several heartbeats.

"Why did you come after us?"

"Beo Hunner an Fie Kews say easy. Kew man wid ba' foot. All tay womun."

"What do you think we should do with him?" Red Petal looked at Redbone.

"It would not sit right with me to kill a man so helpless. But we cannot take him back to his village. We need to be far away from here before anyone finds him."

"If we do not do something with these bodies soon, there will be vultures all over them. They will be easy to find then. The softest ground is in the creek channel. We could bury them in a very shallow grave and maybe the vultures will not get them, but the wolves and coyotes will dig them up quickly."

She kneeled down beside the wounded warrior again. "What is your name?"

"Otter," he said weakly.

"We are going to bury your friends in the muddy creek bottom. It will not keep the wolves and coyotes from getting to them, but maybe it will keep the vultures away for a day or so. We will leave after dark. It may take some time for your clan to find you. I can kill you now if you do not want to suffer."

He looked at her through slitted eyes, pain sweat pouring from his face. "Kew now," he said. He did not want to suffer the excruciating pain in his ruined testicles any longer.

"Your wish," she said as she unhooked her war club.

His eyes opened wide as he saw the club coming at his head. He closed his eyes, felt a sharp pain, and was gone.

"I will dig out your spade, drag our friends into the creek channel, and get some dirt over them. You rest. We should make a poultice to get your arm healed faster."

"I will help you."

"No. You need all your strength to heal. I want you healthy as soon as possible, my man."

After she had all five of them barely covered with the muddy soil, she dragged their canoe over the grave and wrestled it over them. It had high ends, so would not lay flat but it was better than nothing.

By the time she was finished, she was filthy and sweaty. She decided to go find a pool of water to wash up. When she got back, he had the bedding rolled up and ready to load. He also had a green paste on a clean rabbit skin and ready to tie on his bruised arm.

"You have been busy."

"I was feeling useless. Watching you work so hard was too much for me."

She looked at the darkening sky. "Will you be able to get in the canoe?"

"Yes, I can work one-handed tonight. All we need to do is keep from crashing. The current is still fast. We will make good time. But will you be all right? You have not slept, and you have done all that work. You must be ready to drop."

"I will be all right if we do not have any more trouble. It hit me when I was washing up that those were the first men I have ever killed. It did not bother me in the least when it was going on, but I lay in that creek shaking like a leaf. I almost called you to come and hold me."

"You should have." Darkness was on them. "Shall we go?"

He took his seat in the rear of the canoe, and she pushed it down the channel toward the river. She climbed in and practically collapsed into her cramped seat. But she had packs at her back that would make her more comfortable. It was awkward for him to get the canoe backed around and pointed downriver, but they were soon moving in the right direction.

They saw only a few fires flickering on the north side that night. When they finally got settled into a campsite, both were too exhausted to post guard duty, and they just let it go. Sleep came easy for both, and they were not disturbed.

As the days and nights passed, he got stronger, and they went back to posting guard duty each day. A few times, they saw hunters in the woods, but they had no more encounters with warriors.

One night as they were floating along, Redbone noticed the current was getting faster and stronger. "I think we are coming to the rapids Traveler told me about. He said if we stay to the left side, a small channel big enough for a canoe splits off and bypasses the rapids. If we take that, we will not have to portage around the rapids. Keep your eyes focused on that left bank. When you see the opening, paddle hard for the center of it. The space will be tight, but Traveler says we will fit through it."

The roar of the rapids soon dominated all else. Communication was nonexistent. In the starlight, Red Petal saw the opening and paddled hard to get the front of the craft pointed into it. Redbone brought the back around, and they shot through the narrow channel and followed it for what seemed like an eternity. They bounced around as the channel made a few turns, but suddenly they pushed out into a wide, slow pool.

"We made it!" Red Petal cheered.

"Quiet," he admonished her. A large village behind a palisade showed on the north side of the river. "We are not out of the Illini lands yet."

She felt foolish, but no one seemed to hear, and there was no pursuit. They made their way down-river at a more leisurely pace once they passed the rapids. Soon they were in a place of deep forests. Buzzing and biting insects became more of a problem with each passing hand of time. Each night they smeared bear grease with crushed cedar berries over every tiny spot of exposed skin. The nights were warm, humid, and still. The only air movement was what they made by paddling. But any excursion induced heavy sweating, which, in turn, washed off the bear grease mixture, which gave the insects an opening to attack.

The river seemed to wind around continuously, often bending around on itself so that it was difficult to tell what direction they were moving. The darkness seemed to close in on them in those big forests. The channels that drained the forests were as wide as the river, and it took extreme diligence to stay within the river channel.

The ground in the entire area was wet and

marshy. Making a dry camp to sleep in the day became harder. Some days they just tied the canoe off and slept in it in some backchannel. Most days just keeping the insects at bay was the most difficult task. Columns of gossamer wings seemed to climb to the tops of the huge trees.

Though they were always hidden from the river during the daytimes, they were often awakened by conversations in passing canoes. They could never see the occupants, or understand the words spoken, but river traffic was definitely picking up.

One night, they passed a large river coming in from the north. That increased the flow somewhat. Three nights later, another large river came in from the south. Traveler had told him once they passed that river, it would be safe to travel during the day. They would simply blend in with the traffic headed for the Grandfather River.

Two days after the river from the south, they were among a large group of boats that had shifted to the right side of the river. Soon, The Grandfather River came into view. Red Petal was amazed at the amount of water they had encountered. *It seems all the water in the world is right here.* Then she remembered the Great Ocean and marveled at how much water there actually is. *It is like the great turtle is still rising, and the water is still running off.*

They stayed with the group of canoes that took the right fork. Redbone started to question everything he had heard. *This Grandfather River is not nearly as big as the Spirit River. I thought it was the largest river of them all.* Then they cleared an island, and his eyes opened wide. *The grandfather is truly the father of all waters.*

CHAPTER 18
CAHOKIA

Redbone and Red Petal had to work harder than ever to make headway up the Grandfather River. The current relentlessly pushed against the hull of their canoe, trying to make them give up and ride with the flow. But they worked tired muscles to the point of exhaustion, then they worked some more.

"I look forward to feeling your hands rubbing my tired muscles tonight, husband!" Red Petal was anxiously looking for a suitable campsite to duck into for the night, but it seemed there were crowds of people already using every plot of open land. Many canoes lined the bank as they worked their way north. When she saw an open plot, she did not even ask Redbone, she just made for it.

The place where they set their tent up was like a community. All the nearby wood had been scavenged, so they made no attempt to have a hot meal or hot tea. It was a long walk to the closest screening vegetation for use as a latrine. They made that walk together, not knowing what to expect. Any modesty between them had long vanished, but in front of all these strangers?

It did not take long to see that all those people were so used to so many, they paid no attention to anyone but their own little group. There was no organization, and no one seemed to care. They were just many people with one destination in mind—Cahokia.

Redbone finally found a trader who used a trader pigeon he could communicate with. He learned it would take six days from where they were to reach the new canoe landing. The old landing on Cahokia Creek was full all the time, so a newer landing, right on the river was now the only one to use. For a few shells or a necklace, Redbone could hire one of many who haul belongings and freight from the canoe landing to the center of the city. Four to five hands of time was needed to walk there, depending on traffic. These days traffic was heavy every day.

The trader told Redbone everyone wants to be in Cahokia when the great miracle appears. When it does, it will signal the beginning of the requickening of the Morning Star into the body of the son of the Great Sun. When that happens, Cahokia will be ruled by a living god from the sun temple.

"What is the miracle?" Red Petal asked.

"I have no idea, but supposedly we will all know.

The trader says there will be days of ceremonies, pageants, and spectacles. He said this is the best time in history to be a trader in Cahokia. He said there is a row of trader booths along the plaza available for no charge. We just have to be there at the right time to get one. He said not to fear though, because traders just set up and trade their wares all around the Great Plaza. It must be something to see."

"I cannot wait. But first, I want to go in that tent and let you rub my aching shoulders until I roll you over and make love to you like never before."

"That I must experience. Any better than you have already done would be a miracle in itself."

She stood, took his hand, and said, "What are we waiting for?"

"What about all these people?"

"Well, if they had not done what we are about to do, there would not be so many of them, would there?"

Her mischievous smile caused his manhood to go hard. Inside the tent, she was stripped before he had the flap closed. She met him as he walked in and started to undress him.

"Allow me," she said in her "I want you" voice. As she undressed him, she kissed him and rubbed her hardened nipples across his chest. He whimpered around their tongues and into her mouth. She did the same when he fondled her breasts.

"You were supposed to be rubbing my shoulders," she whispered in that deep voice.

"Do you want me to stop this?"

"Never."

By sunrise they were packed, loaded, and ready to start out. Again, they just fell in line with other canoes and started north. They paddled all day, finally stopping with another trader. In sign and pigeon, Redbone learned he had traded along the Tenasee River. That was the big river they passed that came in from the south two days before the grandfather. He had traded on the Great Crab Bay and knew Blue Deer. He was pleased to meet someone who was friends with the man.

For the next four days, Red Petal and Redbone traveled with Farwalker. Late in the afternoon, they found two slots open on the huge Cahokian canoe landing. It was decided to find lodging for the night and start for the city in the morning. For a red fox pelt, Redbone got them a corner of a warehouse where they could store the trade packs and lay out their bedrolls.

The next morning, Redbone and Farwalker contracted to have their trade packs hauled to the Grand Plaza. The traders would follow to the trade booths.

While Redbone and Farwalker talked and signed as they moved toward the great city, Red Petal took in the amazing sights. Within two hands of time, she could make out the main center of the city. They had been passing a mishmash of mounds, warehouses, temples, plazas, and houses all morning. But now, the big mound was coming into view. Below it were other large mounds with temples sitting atop them. East of one pair of mounds on the left side of the road they were on was a large field. In that field was a circle of newly erected poles, with one pole in the center. She had no idea of the purpose of such a thing.

A few of the mounds were round and came to a point. Why? She had no idea. Many of the mounds rose up to a level and were flat. Most of those had a building with a tall, thatched roof on top. Most of those had a fence around what looked like a court-yard outside the building. A tall pole was usually close to the building. Some mounds rose from the ground to a certain height and were level, then a second mound rose from that level area. The second mound would rise up, level off and a building sat on that. It was all very confusing.

As they approached the city center, the wonders increased. Of course, the most noticeable wonder was the giant mound rising from the north end of the plaza. A long line of people were bringing baskets from a borrow pit up the long set of steps set in the south face of the great mound, first to one level, then up more steps to a higher level. The lower level appeared finished, and it had a small building off to one side on a slightly raised mound. *How high will they build it? How high can they build it? That is where their god will live? It is beyond anything I expected. So many mounds. So many people. How can they feed them all?*

They approached the Grand Plaza. Even it was amazing. Red Petal noted the tallest pole she had ever seen standing in the middle of a grassless square in the Grand Plaza. The pole was in line with the center of the steps on the huge mound.

The freight haulers turned right at the edge of the plaza and proceeded south. About halfway down the plaza started a row of booths that went all the way to the south end. The haulers carried the trader packs on a flat rack until they came to two booths next to each other that were unoccupied. They set the racks down and indicated to Redbone and Farwalker to unload them. Red Petal pitched in and helped Redbone get his packs moved into their booth.

The entire afternoon lay in front of them, so Red Petal began opening packs and putting sample items on display around the booth. Soon she discovered that behind the back wall of the booth was living quarters for each trader. She brought their bedrolls and personal items into the living quarters. After that, she went back to putting trade goods on display.

Trading was slow as the afternoon dragged on. At last, the sun set, and they closed down their booth, ate some of the stew and drank the tea Red Petal had prepared in the quiet hours.

Before sunup the next morning, Redbone and

Red Petal were setting up the booth when a conch shell horn blew from the first level of the great mound. A man dressed in some sort of regalia stood at the top of the steps, made some announcement, and pointed to a place in the sky.

Redbone looked to the sky. He looked for several heartbeats before he quietly said, "It truly is a miracle."

"What is?" Red Petal asked.

"The light. See the light in the sky?" He pointed to the shiny dot in the sky.

Farwalker walked up. "This will be a special day for Cahokia," he signed, and pointed to the sky.

Redbone was getting frustrated with the language barrier. He signed "What?" to Farwalker.

The trader pointed to the dot in the sky. "Sign... Morning Star... Come true... New day."

"We are here to witness it, Red Petal! This could be the greatest day the world had ever known. A living god is going to come to the earth and live among men. We will have a story for our grandchildren!"

"I did not know we were having grandchildren?" She said it as a question.

"That matters not. This is big. That 'Guest Star' is going to come down and live right on that mound over there. Cahokia truly is amazing."

"I did not know anything about any of this. I am not sure how important it is in the world we came from."

"You must understand. This is a real god, and he is coming to live in the body of a human being. Cahokia will become the center of all the world."

"Redbone, you are the center of my world. That is what matters to me. I am not interested in this world. It may be a great day for this city, but honestly, that means little to me."

"And you are the center of mine. You are right. What matters is us." He walked over and kissed her.

Farwalker and another man came to Redbone's booth.

"Farwalker tells me you are having a hard time communicating with anyone here. I am Lost Hawk, trader of all nations."

"It is nice to hear a familiar tongue. We came down the Spirit River and have had no one we could talk to for many days. I am Redbone, and this is my wife, Red Petal. She is Lenni Lenape. I am Mononga-hela. We are honored to meet you, Lost Hawk."

"I have known a few traders who took their wives on the rivers, but it is rare. I wish the best for you both. How long will you be here?"

"We really do not know. Ultimately, we would like to see the Shining Mountains, do some trading among the nations in that region. Have you been that way?"

"Of course. Not many places I have not been. I will introduce you to a Shoshone trader. I think he will be glad to guide you to the mountains."

"Have you been to a place called Greenland?"

"Never heard of it. Why?"

"Long story. Probably only interesting to me. Are you in one of these booths?"

"Yes. A ways down the line. Farwalker said you may need some help with tongues. This place will be a madhouse for a time. The trading should be good. If you need me, Farwalker can find me."

"I cannot express how much I appreciate the help."

"Honored to meet you, Lost Hawk." Red Petal lifted her hand, palm up as she voiced her greeting.

People started to take an interest in the trades. More people came by, and soon Redbone and Red Petal were doing a brisk business. Redbone handled most of the men while Red Petal took care of the female customers. By evening, they had few of their original goods left but had more volume than they started out with. Redbone was happy to take in several soft pronghorn pelts and buffalo horns. He also had some grizzly bear claws and a few obsidian blanks.

The next day, the conch shell sounded again, later in the morning this time. It was followed by drums, flutes, and costumed dancers on the terrace of the huge mound. The line of people carrying packs of soil up the stairs did not appear. The dancing carried on with other participants coming and going for more than a hand of time. Finally, the drums silenced, their echoes fading through the trees and distant bluffs.

A group of people walked forward to the top of the steps. They were too distant for Redbone to see if they were men, women, or mixed. They wore white robes with red fringe trim across the shoulders and from the neck to the bottom, just above the ground level. They all wore some sort of colorful headdress and what looked like a forelock held by brightly colored beads. The robes were split in front, but the fringed flap covered them completely. A hand protruded from the front flap and held a colorful staff.

A leader stepped to the front and started some sort of a long speech. At various times during the speech, the thousands of people gathered in the Grand Plaza let out a deafening cheer that was probably heard for great distances.

Redbone and his wife were mesmerized by what they were witnessing. They had never seen anything close to such a spectacle.

When the speaker finally ended his oration, an elaborately decorated older man was brought forward by a much younger man, also elaborately dressed, gripping the older man's elbow. Both men had partially painted faces and some design around their eyes. Each man wore a tall headdress and sported a beaded forelock. The older man's forelock appeared red while the younger man's was bright yellow.

The crowd roared when the two stepped to the edge of the steps. When the crowd settled down, the older man began a speech, but his voice did not carry to Redbone's ears. He would not understand the tongue anyway. A few times during the speech, the crowds roared again. When the speech ended, the younger man raised his arms high, revealing a wing-like webbing under each arm. The crowd went wild as the two men turned and walked stately out of sight toward the back of the terrace.

"I know not what he said, but he sure stirred up the people." Red Petal looked at Redbone with wonder in her eyes.

"Yes, I wonder who they were."

As the massive crowd began to disperse, many started perusing the wares displayed by the traders. Throughout the day the couple traded each of their items for something more exotic to them. By the end of the day, they had completely changed their inventory at least twice.

Lost Hawk invited them to go meet and have evening meal with Sheep Talker, the Shoshone trader he had told Redbone about earlier. The trader had a firepit behind his booth that was bigger than most. Up to ten people could sit around it on log pieces Sheep Talker had brought in. Lost Hawk made the introductions, and by surprise, Sheep Talker could use the Lenape tongue.

"You have come far," Sheep Talker said to Redbone.

"Yes, and my wife has come farther," Redbone replied.

"Lost Hawk tells me you are interested in seeing the Shining Mountains. Do you know anything about them?"

"Not really. A friend was born somewhere on a river out that way. He told me a few things. He is an old trader who spent much time around Cahokia."

"What is this trader called?" When Sheep Talker asked the question, Lost Hawk perked up.

"Traveler is the only name he has ever known, he says."

"Traveler still breathes? How old is he?" Sheep Talker asked.

"He does not know. Said when he was found, he could not talk, maybe not even walk. All he knows, it was somewhere far up the Grandmother River. I expect he has seen more than six tens and five summers."

"I heard he quit the trade and settled down with some Head Matron, somewhere in the east."

"You heard right. The Head Matron of Mononga-hela Village accepted him as her fourth husband, The other three had died. She died nearly two sun cycles past."

While they were talking, a young woman who wore a dress made from tanned pronghorn skins brought plates of food to everyone. It was dark-colored and had painted decorations of strange symbols. Her black hair was loose and hung to her waist. Her round face had pretty features highlighted by large, round eyes.

"Allow me to introduce my daughter, Meadow Dew. This is her first venture to Cahokia. She has seen ten-and-four-summers, and her mother thinks she is too young to go so far from home. Says she needs to stay home and find a husband. I say she needs to see something of the world before she gets married," Sheep Talker explained.

Meadow Dew blushed. She obviously understood the Lenape tongue.

"Meadow Dew, this is Redbone and Red Petal, who have come all the way from the Lenape lands, far to the east of here," Sheep Talker told his daughter.

"We are honored to make your acquaintance, Meadow Dew," Red Petal told the young maiden.

"This meat is delicious. What is it?" Redbone asked as he savored the meaty stew he was eating.

"Pronghorn. Some say they do not care for it, but they just do not know how to cook it, I think," replied Sheep Talker.

"Dew will not have a difficult time finding a husband if she can cook like this!" Red Petal pointed at her empty bowl.

"I had planned to stay here three more days, but I have completely turned over my inventory. I can be ready to head back toward the mountains tomorrow morning, if you want me to guide you there. We cannot get all the way to Tall Ram's camp before winter. I know a Comanche village where we can winter," said Sheep Talker.

"We need to talk it over. We have turned over our inventory at least twice, just today," Redbone answered as he looked to Red Petal for reaction.

"I would be more than happy to leave this place. Too many people for my liking, too many lecherous looks from too many strange-looking men. I will take my chances with winter," Red Petal offered.

"Then it is settled. When does the cold maker invade your country?" Redbone asked.

"Anytime. But hot weather can also come at any time. Our people must always be prepared for any kind of weather."

"Sounds interesting."

Shortly after sunrise, they were negotiating to have their packs hauled to the canoe landing.

CHAPTER 19

THE SHINING MOUNTAINS

Sheep Talker led them up the Grandmother River. They encountered many water hazards, such as snags, sawyers, whirlpools, high water from summer storms, and rocky shoals. Red Petal proved her worth, avoiding the dangers or warning Redbone every time. She became fit and strong, relishing the hard work.

Sheep Talker stressed that their party should make it to a Comanche village whose chief was a good friend, before winter. But beware, the Comanche are traditional enemies of the Shoshone, and if they run into the wrong camp, there could be trouble.

"We are no strangers to warfare, and have dealt with our share of enemies, my friend," said Redbone.

"Yes, but winter in your lands is not the same as winter in the mountains, even worse on the plains. The chances of surviving a winter outside of a friendly village are very low. We will face much danger if we do not find Bull Heart. It is not possible to get all the way to Tall Ram's camp."

"How long will it take us to get to Bull Heart's village?"

"We should get there in time to help with the fall buffalo hunt. By helping, we will be more welcome than if we arrive late."

"Let us go!" Red Petal joined the conversation. She had just returned from relieving her bladder and had not heard the whole talk.

"Be careful what you wish for, Red Petal. Among the Comanche, women only skin and butcher the animals. It is bloody and back-breaking work."

"If I..."

"They will not let you in on the hunt. If they set up a jump, you can be part of the living fence, which is very dangerous. Then sorting through the dead and live animals after the drive can be deadly. Better to hope we surround them in open ground and hope one does not decide to run over you when the shooting starts."

"You make it sound like a picnic."

"Just do not want you to have any delusions."

"Thank you. I will be ready."

"All right, let us load up. We still have ten days before we reach the Meneo 'he' 'e."

Red Petal and Meadow Dew made a pact to work extra hard paddling up the Grandmother River, and they reached the Meneo 'he' 'e a full day sooner than Sheep Talker predicted.

At the confluence, they met a band of Omaha hunters who had mounds of deer meat piled on dog travois they were hauling back to their village. The party of five hunters became very interested when they saw two women in the canoes.

The Omaha leader came to Sheep Talker and signed that he would trade meat for a turn with the women for him and his men.

Sheep Talker signed "No." The offer was upped. The answer stayed "No." One of the Omaha had eased closer to Redbone's canoe. He started to reach for Red Petal's hair. She was ready and drove her paddle into his gut, driving the wind from him.

The other Omaha pulled warclubs and started to charge toward the beached canoes, but when they saw paddles prepared to do more damage they backed off.

Sheep Talker signed "a fool thinks a woman is defenseless...take meat and go to village."

The second in charge nodded his head and spoke to the wounded one. They turned to a trail headed east over the bluff.

The canoes paddled hard, putting as much distance between them and the Omaha village as possible. They posted guards at night, keeping cold camps, but were never followed.

The days were hot and dry. The water in this river had a slightly bitter taste so they hunted fresh water springs where small creeks ran into it. After a rare rain shower, the Meneo 'he' 'e cleared up for a day or two, but then they had to look for fresh water springs again.

One day Red Petal impressed Sheep Talker when she dropped a mule deer doe more than fifty paces distant. They ate fresh meat for a two days and smoked the rest while they rejuvenated their bodies by laying in the warm, shallow water, or just resting.

One night, after a rollicking lovemaking session. Red Petal was lying half on Redbone catching her breath.

"Have you ever thought about what it would be like to be a father?"

"Am I going to be one?" he asked sharply.

"Not from me, not now! If that is what you are worried about. I was just curious. We have been together for more than a sun cycle now, and I was curious is all. We have never talked about it."

"I told my mother we will never have children. I would not want to bring one into the world with a foot like this, or some other damaged part."

"That is a worry every parent must face. Are you saying there should be no more children because one might be damaged someday, even though tens of tens of tens are born without that kind of damage? What happens when all the children grow old and die? What will happen then?"

"You sound like you want children. How could we manage a child right now?"

"Not now. Not when we are doing this. But some-day, yes, I want to give you a son...and a daughter would be fun, too. Just not right now."

"We will see. Right now, we need sleep. Tomorrow will be a long day, and we both have guard duty later. Good night, my love."

"I love you with all my souls, Redbone. Promise you will never leave me."

"Never!"

She leaned up and kissed him on the cheek, then slid down with her back against his warm body.

The Meneo 'he' 'e was shallow, slow moving in places, fast in others. It flowed in several channels that divided, twisted, turned, rejoined, and divided again. Some places, the main channel was difficult to follow, and it changed with each spring, so it was not practical to rely on memory. Taking the wrong braid could end up in a dead end or a feeder creek. Sheep Talker had to be alert so he could read the river and tell Meadow Dew where to make her course corrections. Red Petal only needed to follow the craft in front of her.

The endless, unchanging plains added to the monotonous paddling day after day. They came to a place where the river divided, and it looked to Redbone that the right fork was the best, but Sheep Talker took the left fork. It took Redbone two days to realize the experienced man knew the best route.

Six days later, they came to another fork. This time, Sheep Talker took the right fork and confused

Redbone again, but he kept his mouth shut. Not far up that fork, they encountered a grizzly bear. The animal appeared to be hunting on the north side of the river and took a keen interest in the unusual sight of humans. He watched them go by, but did not pursue, for which they were all thankful. Redbone tried to guess how much fat could be rendered from a bear that big.

As they progressed, they noted the weather getting cooler, especially each night. One morning they woke up to a coating of frost on every surface. Leggings and heavy shirts became the norm, although a day here or there would surprise them, and the heavy clothes came off.

Finally, some unusual topography began to show. There was a spire rock formation, then a large, chunky formation back from the river. The following morning, a huge formation that resulted in the river flowing faster as it twisted and turned through a canyon with high, vertical cliffs. Then they were past that and back in the plains. But now they could see mountains.

The change stimulated them into working harder. They rounded a bend, and there were five warriors in front of them. The warriors stood with strung bows and nocked arrows. They were spread out and had the river channel covered. One of the warriors waved them to the bank where they waited. As soon as they stopped, the warriors came forward, pointing the arrows at them.

"Aho, Sheep Talker, friend of the Comanche, seeks Bull Heart, brave leader of men."

"Sheep Talker will find no friends in the village of Dancing Buffalo. Step out of the canoe, one at a time, men first."

Redbone and Red Petal had been learning Comanche from Sheep Talker since they left Cahokia and were well versed in it. They both knew they were overmatched and would have to do as they were told.

The warriors laughed when they saw Redbone hobbling on his bad foot. His warclub and knife were taken and tucked into one of the warrior's waist belt. Next he and Sheep Talker had their arms pulled back and tied at the elbows and wrists behind their backs.

Three of the warriors then turned their attention to the women. Meadow Dew was roughly pulled from the canoe. They pushed her toward Sheep Talker, but not before one of them grabbed her breast and laughed. Once next to Sheep Talker, they looped a long rope over her head and pulled it tight around her neck. Again, one grabbed her breast, twisted, and laughed. Next they tied her wrists behind her back. Two came over to Red Petal.

Redbone was wishing he had never brought Red Petal to this part of the world. He felt helpless and stupid.

The two warriors took Red Petal by the arms and pulled her out of the canoe. When they felt her muscular arms, they began to check the rest of her anatomy. They quickly tied her hands behind her back. They each took a breast, squeezing and twisting painfully. She did not let on that it hurt. She looked at Redbone and saw the remorse in his eyes.

"I am all right," she said in the Monongahela tongue.

A warrior cuffed her on the back of the head and said, "Do not use words!"

Next, a long rope was looped over her head and pulled tight around her neck.

"Follow!" the leader told them.

He led the way along a trail. One warrior took Red Petal's neck rope, and another took Meadow Dew's. Red Petal could tell they had nothing but disdain for Meadow Dew. She was not sure how they felt about her.

The trail went around the shoulder of a hill and fell away into a wide, shallow valley. In the valley was the village of around three tens of conical-shaped lodges.

Red Petal could hear the warriors behind her talking rudely to Redbone and Sheep Talker. Twice, she heard Redbone stumble and fall. Each time, he was hauled back to his feet and shoved forward.

The leader took them to the largest lodge in the village. A big man stepped out. He had seen more than three tens of years. His face was scared and ugly. He wore a red fringed shirt with some broken quill chevrons on the chest. Several of the fringe strings were missing or shorter than the others. He wore a dark-brown breechclout and worn brown leggings with half the fringe strings missing. His moccasins appeared nearly new and were well made.

He walked up to Sheep Talker and said, "We meet again, Sheep Talker. Tell me why I should spare you. You are trespassing on Comanche land. This is not the first time, but it could be the last."

"Dancing Buffalo, Sheep Talker does not and has never taken animals from your lands. He merely passes through to make trade in far places. Sheep Talker is a trader of all nations and is protected by the Power of Trade."

"Here you are, on our land, with not enough time to get to your worm-ridden Shoshone village before winter. How did you plan to not kill our game and still live through the winter?"

"Sheep Talker planned to find the village of Bull Heart and winter with his friend. I am guiding these Lenni Lenape and Monongahela People into the mountains that may offer their wares to the people. They, too are protected by the Power of Trade."

"They are trespassers, as you are. But this woman is most handsome. Perhaps I will trade the clubfoot's life for his woman. She would make a fine addition to my lodge." He reached up and slid fingers across her chin and lips.

She said nothing but looked at him with hate in her eyes.

"And this one? She is your daughter?"

"Yes, I took her to Cahokia to teach her the trade."

"It gets late. I will decide your fate tomorrow. This woman will share the blankets of Dancing Buffalo this night. The girl will sleep with my other wives. You *traders* will sleep out here. I will not waste heat on trespassers."

"Red Petal is my wife and not for trade. Do not touch her!" Redbone could not stop himself from threatening the chief.

"Another outburst, and you will be sleeping with your ancestors," Dancing Buffalo told Redbone.

"Put two guards on each of them, take them some place where I will not need to listen to his whining. Do not disturb me."

A LOOK AT BOOK EIGHT
BRIGHT MOON

A warrior forged by courage must stand against a storm of enemies and betrayal.

Bright Moon has always been different from the other girls in her village. While they tend to hearth and home, she has spent her life training as a hunter and protector. Her sharp instincts and unconventional strategies earning the admiration—and envy—of even the most experienced warriors.

Now, as Haudenosaunee raids grow more ruthless, Bright Moon is thrust into the fight of her life. The enemy's war chief is no ordinary adversary. He's as clever as he is relentless and will stop at nothing to destroy her village. His most dangerous weapon? A spy—his own daughter—sent to infiltrate Bright Moon's defenses and unearth the secrets that could bring her people to ruin.

Haunted by strange, vivid dreams that connect her to her brother, Redbone, and his wife, Red Petal, as they face perils of their own in distant lands, Bright Moon must navigate not only the physical battlefield but also the uncertain terrain of her heart and spirit.

AVAILABLE APRIL 2025

ABOUT THE AUTHOR

Ron Briggs is a veteran, having served four years in the USAF. His education includes a Bachelor of Science in Range and Wildlife Ecology at Oklahoma State University and a Master of Science in Range and Wildlife Management at Texas A&I University.

He is retired from the USDA-Natural Resources Conservation Service, and his career encompassed twenty-five years as District Conservationist in Linn County, Kansas. Prior to college, he worked seven years in the building trades.

Having developed a deep interest in history, especially in the pre-colonial period of North America, Ron's interests prompted him to begin researching a pre-history story about the Tallgrass Prairie Region of the Great Plains. That research evolved into his current multi-volume work, the Yellow Hair series, which includes scenes from northern Europe to the mountains of western North America.

Ron and his wife, Debbie, currently live in Mound City, Kansas, and have two grown children and seven grandchildren. His interests include spending time with family, writing, hunting, fishing, traveling, and woodworking.

www.ingramcontent.com/pod-product-compliance
Lightning Source LLC
Chambersburg PA
CBHW021843130726
47989CB00009B/3061